PUDDING STONE

Puddingstone
Copyright © 2014 by Mark Jay Mirsky. All rights reserved.

ISBN: 978-0-9906254-0-7

For my son, Israel Mirsky, whose steadfast interest in the world of this novel led to my resolve to see it both as a digital publication and in print.

The graphics throughout this edition are the work of
Inger Johanne Grytting

Cover design by Stewart A. Williams

Franklin Park in 1965

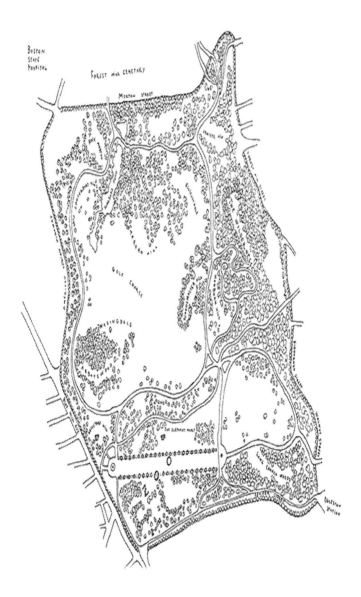

x

Excerpts of *Puddingstone* appeared in the magazines, *Moment*, *Fiction*, and *Heal*.

Franklin Park

PUDDING STONE

A novel by

Mark Jay Mirsky

Fog

In a **Boston lost** in the fog of the sixties …

Mirl's Mother

Maishe Ostropol *Mirl*

Why did <u>he</u> leave <u>his wife</u> behind? That's what I want to know. Because, believe me, right from the beginning I knew that Maishe Ostropol was a faker, a B student at the Sarah Greenwood Elementary, never mind Harvard, Shmarvard—my Mirl was making a fool of him in the kindergarten, and believe me, old as I am, my teeth haven't fallen out, yet was I surprised when that *pisher*[1] shows up here in Newton as the rabbi, all right it's not an Orthodox shul,[2] you know, fancy pancy, my Max could hardly afford the initiation fee, five thousand, no fooling with Hebrew, intellectual, a bunch of names that would break your mouth every Friday night from the pulpit from that *pisher*, who knew what he was talking about, but like Max says, the steam room, the *whatchyoucallit*, "sauna," terrific, and the biggest pool in Newton, triple Olympic, with a special masseuse, Finnish *shiksa*, 100 percent, so don't complain, it's all on the up and up, but I knew the first moment I laid eyes on that faker it was 110 percent

[1] young insignificant person; squirt Yiddish: bed-wetter
[2] synagogue

unkosher baloney, a big one, in his mouth, you think I don't know him—and that wife!

I went right over, introducing, "I knew your Maishe, when my Mirl," and right away we hit it off, so take the baloney out of your mouth; but no, a bigger one; I told her, "Honey, you got to hold on to a *bubbemeiser* like that by the *gutchkies*," but talk, talk, talk, all the time, he disappears in a cloud of it, right out of the kitchen by his own wife, and I'm sitting there, ignoring me? I never said a word of what I knew to anyone, a *confidante* I was, to this moment, a safe, my mouth, I threw away the combination, how he locked his room with a key so she shouldn't get in and even the keyhole, Scotch taped, carried in his pocket, she shouldn't throw it away, and a ladder to get out of the back window and run all over who knows where without his yarmulke, and that special study group he wouldn't let her come to, *nu*, she inhibited him, that kind of talk, talk, talk, to me too, "out of my kitchen," when I interrupted, "My Mirl …" he shouted at me and she, right back told him, "It's *my* kitchen," and then (I'm ashamed to tell you), language from the other side, the tracks, the same Maishe from kindergarten, screaming, yelling, all purple, smacking her and showing me the kitchen knife, I could have sued!

He grabs me by the hand. "Stick it in," he whispers, putting the point right to his Adam's apple, "it's *your* kitchen, you want the fatted calf?" Right away, I saw he was crazy and I told her, "Mattapan, call Mattapan," but she goes nutty too. "Leave," she is crying, "leave, please Mrs., leave!" I should have known right then, get out, out of the sauna, the steam bath, the swimming pool, the sunroom with Max in his underwear. I should have run right out of that temple and a million miles away to Brookline or *Zaide's* shul in Brighton, never mind I didn't understand a word because right then I made my mistake, *me ken mishuggeh veren*. I thought, a friend, she needs a friend, her own age, it's a *machaiah*, a *mitzvah*, I'm not going to leave the *maidle* in despair, my Mirl will make ... So I started it, me, Max said, me, from the hospital bed he's shaking his finger at me. I don't have enough aggravation. I haven't got ulcers, piles, kidney stones? All right, my heart is too big. I didn't have an attack. Max, what do I have to do, rip off my bra to show the pain, the ache, you want a naked lady running around the Beth Israel, *Gottenyu*? Enough. My Mirl! My Mirl!

A happy married lady with kids, I brought her over from a split-level ranch house in Brookline, a real synagogue, Conservative, to join this House of Gomorrah. "Get in with him," I said. "Join that study group. Find out what's going on. She needs help. And the pool ... We'll pay the difference. It's just terrific. We'll all be in it together. A *sauna*, you know, hot water."

Bernie, the husband, the doctor, comes over. "What's with Mirl? Momma, first the talk, talk talk ..." (my heart goes bad like an old herring when I hear that, the talk, talk, talk) then the short skirts, the separate room, a new key, Scotch tape (Oy vey, the Scotch tape, tape, tape) "Mirl, sweetheart," I asked her, "Is that *Maishe Pisher,* the little boy who wet his pants in kindergarten, who couldn't even pin the tail on the donkey, leading you around by the nose?" "Momma, please, we all grow up." "Grow up? So why do you run around like a baby with your knees showing? The doctor …" "Never mind with the doctor, please, he sees plenty of knees."

"Knees, so, he's a doctor, but the Rabbi."

"Never mind with the Rabbi."

"Never mind with the Rabbi? Listen, Mirl, your momma …"

"Momma, I'm already a momma, so never mind with the 'Momma,' " and right like that she walks out of her own kitchen on me into the bedroom and turns the key. "What's with the talk, talk, talk," I got to shout through a closed door. And I don't get a peep.

I got to call Mattapan for my own daughter. The doctor is supposed to fix everything. Everything, he tells me, but this and puts his finger in his ear. "I can't fix the talk, talk, talk." "Max! You got to speak to her, Max!" Only Max right away starts in on me, that it's me who started with the talk, talk, talk. Good and loud right in front of the husband, the doctor, so she can hear it right through the Scotch tape that I'm the original talk, talk, talk, until I'm so mixed up I got to start yelling, am I the one who runs out on her husband, who climbs down ladders, who's running all over Roxbury looking for the Queen of Sheba. Did I love on the wrong side of the tracks or pee in my pants or pin the tail on myself, or show my *pishy* in the cloakroom so they got to calm me down with a pot of cold water and I can't stop hiccupping?

"It's all right, Momma," only it's not all right, let the doctor fix, why can't the doctor fix it, he'll fix everything. Fix it! Fix it!

Okay, I got excited. Over nothing, nothing! It's nothing, I got to run over and feed my own grandchildren. Running around in dirty underwear. "It's nothing, Momma." "I let you? ..." "You did too much." "Too much? Momma did too much? A new talk, talk, talk!"

She don't feel good now that I sewed up holes in her socks, dresses, stood behind the counter at Max's Five and Dime, she should have the extra special shiny patent leather pumps for kindergarten, made everyday surprises—cookies, cakes—she should have dumplings in her cheeks, spent on music, art, dancing school, a fortune, she should be a little lady, took her every day to first grade, second, third, the boys shouldn't get fresh, made for her friends a home away from home all the way through high school, college, moved special, she should have a better school, nice people to play with, now her kids got to look like little *Maishe pisher* with mud from the drainpipes all over the face playing dirty games with his little sister Essy right across from our front porch in his empty lot? It's natural, Momma, and not even the doctor is going to interfere and Max is afraid to pick up his own grandchildren because they'll get pee-pee all over his nice new suit pants. Only I can't say nothing, because I did too much.

Better I should come myself in dirty underwear, we can all sit in the house and smell of *kakka*? "Mirl, we got to have a talk ..." "No more talk ..." "Mirl, you got to change, you ..." "No, Momma ..." "What do you mean, no Momma? Come here *kindeleh* ... I'm just going to give you a nice sweet … What do you mean, no? No? I brought them myself … my own … look! Straight from the baby shop … no pins … nothing. What do you mean, no? What do you mean, yours … yours, yours? Yours is mine, mine … this is my own … flesh … blood. I'm going to … no? Max! I can't … Max! A crazy house … a Mattapan. I'm calling, I'm calling … the whole family … everyone … Mattapan."

A trip, now she wants me to go on a trip … the nerves … relax … the doctor will pay … time to enjoy … what … what can I enjoy … a change … what can I change? I don't want to change … What's with this change business? She'd like a change, change what, I'm asking …you want to get me out of the way … first with the … then with the change, change, change? "I should have a talk? With who? … No … Mirl … no … with a kid who *pishes* in his pants? I'm supposed to go in and a big lady already make like a? … Mirl, please your momma, she's an old lady, look, her teeth are falling out, fake, all of them rotten. I got a cancer, Mirl, inside me, I know it, my kidneys are all eaten up, my stomach, my liver, and my heart, Mirl, my heart is too big, so stop, stop, with the change, please, Mirl, stop with the change. Nothing, Mirl, nothing's going to change."

Only I'm going to kill him. I'm going back to that kitchen and pick the knife up. A murderer, a demon, I should have stuck it right in. I'm going to kill. Kill, Mirl! Momma, Momma's going to kill him! Heart attack, breakdown, nothing's going to change. I'm promising Mirl. Just get me the doctor. Get me the doctor. I want the doctor. Where's the doctor?

The Messiah's Nose

The dreams of men go on to the Messiah, a new time, a new world or return to a vanished moment to remain there, if possible, forever.

The Messiah calls—abandon time. For that reason the tribe, while affirming the coming of Messiah with the lip, has always been suspicious. A part of the tribe is always fighting to return to old time, its childhood, when the Presence of Divinity was among us and there was no talk of deliverers. Redemption rolling round was daily.

The coming of a new Time—return to an old Time—in the stream the currents battle—the river a whirlpool.

The Hebrew Advocate

April 1, 1948

HERE'S CHAIM!

Ah Dorchester, dear Dorchester and not just Dorchester,
but Mattapan and Roxbury. From
the special at Maxie's, deep in
Grove Hall, an Eden of corned
beef, pickle and potato salad
35 cents, to Maxine's Fluff and
Whirl at the edge of Milton,
the Paradise Permanent $1.50,
this week only, one avenue,
Blue Hill, one people, Jews,
one nation, America, God
Bless!!

Blood Pudding

Late in the afternoon that Sunday, there appeared in Franklin Park Bar Kokhaba, son of star, chasing off Billy Mulvaney, little O'Coogan, White and Reilly; boys who were beating a young Hebrew, age seven, with a two-inch board on the crown of his head unprotected except for the purple stocking cap knitted by his mother.

The lads listened in the morning to a sermon by the Reverend S. J. O'Halloran at Saint Leo's Church off Dorchester's Harvard Street. The priest's sermon on the Messiah and the Jews was a poignant allegory of human evil. Feeling the smart of an historical affront, the lads have been searching for an opportunity to avenge it. Ascertaining Ostropol's religion by the symbol embroidered in his cap, interlocking triangles—and finding him alone—they sprang from behind a fallen maple and drew him deep into the byways of the park, tugging at his frayed coat cuffs, slyly kicking his bum, caressing his ears.

"We guht somethin' to show yuh. Real good. C'mon. What's yuh name? Hey, *Mayshee*, wait'll yuh see it. Down here. C'mon. Oh, excuse me, Mayshee, I didn't mean to. Yooh Jewish right? Yuh? We like 'em. We guht somethin' foh yuh."

Giggles from eight-year-old O'Coogan. Reilly has to clip the baby of the gang across the mouth. Ostropol is starting to slow down, drag, refusing to take steps toward the far reaches of the park, where a deserted stretch of woods rose from the cracks in the pudding-stone. "Yuh gonna see d'dead get up. Huh, don't yuh wanna see it?" Mulvaney opens his green eyes wide on the last consonant, which spit from his tongue.

"My mummy wants me," the Hebrew protests.

"What are yuh," Reilly, the biggest of the boys puts in, "a sissy?"

"Sissy," sings O'Coogan.

"Dere's gold in a cave dere," says Mulvaney, who has begun the talk. "I seen it shinin'. N'all kindsa stuff, yuh can't even believe, like a whole tub'a candy."

"C'mon," says White, the quiet one.

Still the captive stands rooted in the path, straining to hear his mother's voice.

Reilly, descendent of Kerry giants, towers a half-foot over the Hebrew, pushes his fist into Ostropol's lips. "Sissy," he mocks.

"C'mon." White raises his torn brown corduroy, a pink knee bone glinting in its sheath and kicks as hard as he can at Ostropol's cushion of backside.

"Don't yuh like candy?" croons Mulvaney.

"He's ... look ... he's ..." pipes O'Coogan, hopping. The gang looks to the leaves, steaming.

All four sniff to determine if the victim has befouled himself.

"Did yuh?" Reilly growls. "Did yuh?"

"I smell it," O'Coogan screeches. "He did it."

"Whaddayuh scaaid of?" whispers Reilly. "We was just testin' yuh."

"Don't yuh want no candy?" asks Mulvaney.

"C'mon," says Reilly, taking Ostropol by the shoulder. "Y'can't go home till yuh dry out. Yuh mummy'll be mad." He flings over his arm to the gang, "He ain't no sissy."

"Yuhh," all assent as they urge their acquaintance forward, down a long, grassy slope, the sheaves bending like grain, uncut, on into the woods, clambering up a stone wall, over a fence into the Wilderness, the unchartered west of Franklin Park, a place of deep puddles, thickets, shallow caves, puddingstone hollowed out in cones and pits along which Maishe and his captors crawl. They come to a rift in the rock cliff—look down to a far drop, the forest floor below the tops of thick oaks and maples. The gang lowers itself into a crib through a fissure in the conglomerate. They are in a cave, high above the trees, stepping in the ashes of campfires, broken bottles, crate slats. The mouth of the hiding place in the cliff face is stopped up with heavy boards, a barrier propped with charred two-by-fours. A patch of blue sky shows between the top of this wall and the ceiling of the crib.

O'Coogan puts his eye to a knot hole punched out in the barrier.

"Anyone outside?" asks Mulvaney. "Listen." They bend their heads a minute to the wind.

Only the footsteps in the tops of the trees—the company cannot pick out a tread—only the shaking of a cold kiss. A sudden scurry in the leaves below—they start.

"It's a squirrel," whispers O'Coogan.

The crusading host resists an impulse to follow the animal with stones. They turn and look at Ostropol.

Dipping his hands into the trash, Reilly scoops out a pale green rubber, sticks his finger in. He licks his lips at the corner and wiggles it, "Tootsie. Tootsie."

"Know what it is?" asks Mulvaney.

Ostropol wags his head.

The gang smirks. Reilly puts his nose so close to Ostropol that the latter can see tiny red pimples and pockmarks. The lips of the older boy curl. His teeth glisten. "Take yuh pants down, Mayshee."

Mulvaney, O'Coogan, even White, break out in laughter. "Mayshee!"

Ostropol's jaw hangs open but the chords are stuck. "Wan' me to stick my finguh in?" asks Reilly.

Ostropol hears the chuckles scratching in the dry leaves around him, crackling the gold, red, purple flakes.

A green peg slips into his open mouth before he realizes it. He jerks his head away, spits saliva on the ground.

"Hey," says Reilly. "What yuh doin'? Is this yuh house?" He shakes Ostropol by the coat lapel. "Would yuh spit on the floah in yuh house?"

"Apologize," demands Mulvaney.

"I wanna apology!" Reilly barks.

Ostropol stammers, wind in his chest.

"Too late," White cuts him off.

"Take yuh pants down, Mayshee," pipes O'Coogan.

"We wanna check," Mulvaney adds softly. Ostropol twists from face to face.

"Yuh gotta show yoah sorry." Mulvaney steps on O'Coogan's foot, to shut him up. "We don' care. Just don' do it again. We gotta check though.

"We ain't sure yuh tellin' us d'truth," Reilly adds.

"C'mon," White growls, grabbing Ostropol's belt.

"He ain't ready," Mulvaney interrupts.

"Scai'd?" asks White.

"Mayshee, look!" Reilly unhitches the buckle of his thick black leather belt. "See," he points to the shining key of his fly as he draws down the tab of the zipper on a yellow pair of cotton drawers. He steps out of his pants. Ostropol can see the shorts bunched up and streaked in the rear, the elastic limp. They sag down not even covering Reilly's behind. Ostropol looks away.

"Whatsa matter? Yuh afraid? It ain't gonna eat yuh," Reilly laughs.

"Look," White insists.

Ostropol looks back as Reilly pulls down the dirty shorts, snapping the frayed elastic, a zither. The snake springs out from the pants, hooded. "Suck it," Reilly says.

The gang giggles. "Everyone," Reilly orders.

Little O'Coogan, White, Mulvaney, slip their belts out, uncinching the tongue of steel and Maishe Ostropol, heart in his collarbone, follows suit. They sit down on bare rumps, having discarded trousers and underwear, on broken bottle necks, rusty nails, sharp stones, splintered timber. Ostropol is aware that their eyes are on his fringe of flesh.

"How big is it?" asks O'Coogan.

"Tickle it," suggests Mulvaney. "Make it stand up."

"Want me to?" offers O'Coogan.

Ostropol cups his hands over it.

"Hey," threatens White.

"We're showing ours," explains Mulvaney.

Ostropol removed his palms. He placed them down in the rustling leaves.

"It ain't so special," complains O'Coogan.

"Can't yuh do no tricks with it?" asks Mulvaney. "I guht candy foh yuh."

Ostropol shakes his head. His captors look at his— shrunken, half hidden.

"How come yuh don't talk?" asks Reilly.

Mulvaney whispers in his ear, "Wanna hear a story?"

Ostropol does not move his head. "Evah he-uh o'da Save-yuh?"

The Jewish boy nods.

"Whaddyah he-uh?"

"Good things?" squeaks O'Coogan.

"Bad," cut in White. Ostropol, his mouth half open, stops the word that is about to come out.

"Whaddyah he-uh?" repeats Reilly.

A broken bit of brown glass is biting into Maishe's palm, trembling in the wet leaves, seasons of them, rotting on the cave floor.

"He got beat'n up," says Mulvaney.

"They broke his legs," intones Reilly.

"That was nothin'," whispers Mulvaney. "They had this here trial where dey talked all kindsa crazy lies, sayin' dirty things. D'yuh hear about it?"

"I heard," says Reilly.

"They took his pants off'n stahted beatin' him. You evah get hit wid a whip? Nails n'glass, n'all kindsa crap, right a d'tip so it tore right inta duh skin. All puffed out n'horrible. You'd be screamin', Mayshee. O'Coogan show him."

O'Coogan picks his bum out of the leaves and displayed six welts a parental hand had raised there. The scars of a former beating were crusted over.

"They stuck thohns in'm," Mulvaney reminds his audience. "A whole bunch, long, like spikes, right in his head, laughin', tellin'im it was a crown, while blood was spurtin' out of his hair."

Ostropol is looking into green, green eyes, hearing of one covered with scars worse than O'Coogan's, sharp bristles squeezed into his brain.

"They spit." White's phlegm catches Ostropol in his eye.

"Like that," Reilly spits.

"That!" White's second hits Maishe across his lips.

"That?" Little O'Coogan's went wide, flecking Ostropol's eye.

"They slapped him," Mulvaney sings.

"Hard," adds Reilly.

"Hard?" White asks.

"What me to show yuh?" Mulvaney grins.

"No," Ostropol croaks, getting up.

"Siddown," says Reilly, shoving the boy back. Maishe grabs in the leaves for his pants. He has heard the story on the radio. It is a bad one, his mother had told him when he asked. Reilly smacks hard, as hard as he can. A beam slams in Ostropol's face. His fingers clutch the belt of his pants. The green finger of Reilly shakes before him like a gas mask.

"You evah he-uh of d'Save-yuh?" Reilly repeats the question.

"Yuh know who he was?" asks Mulvaney.

"Yuh?" adds White.

"Yuh believe that?" Reilly asks.

"Yuh he-uh of his Muth-ah?"

"Yuh …" White nodded.

"Know what d'Jews did?" Mulvaney continues.

"Dey stuck thohns in'm. Anyone evah stick a thohn? …"

"Stick'm Reilly," squeals O'Coogan. "Stick'm."

The points of four nails flash out of a tight thumb. "Hold'm White. Mulvaney!" Pinned into a bed of leaves, glass, the steel points of nails scratch Ostropol's nose.

"Stick'm," wails O'Coogan.

"He's bleedin'," whispers White.

"Yuh gutta beat'm first." Mulvaney's voice rises. "They took off all his clothes. Naked. Den they scouhged him, they give him somethin' to drink."

Bitter water spatters across Maishe's face. He twists frantic.

White snarls, backing off. "Aim it, O'Coogan."

"He's gettin' away. Hold d'feet. White, hit'm with the boahd. Hit'm White."

The thunderous crack which shook Ostropol did not fall from the two-by-four which little O'Coogan and White slammed down, for Maishe rolled to the side with a jerk and it caught Reilly on the arm. It was the edge of the iron blade, wide as a shovel that had thrust through the boards of the barrier. Snapped by the hand wielding it backwards, the blade shivered the wooden wall of the cave apart.

His tormentors froze as an arm broad as their backs appeared through the hole holding the hilt of a crude Roman short sword. But they did not see over the top of the broken fence, the sun-blackened face of the giant.

Did this figure, breathing burning tow, touch them with the sharp point of his sword?

They do not hear the curse speak from the walls of the cave. As they have done, it shall be done to them. But they jump away from the sound of the blade, bruising elbows, knees, scraping skin; flee up the fissure of the rock, witless; do not recover until running under the lamps of Washington Street, the evening lights blink on. A paddy wagon screeches alongside four boys without pants.

As for Maishe Ostropol, he does not behold the face of Bar Kokhaba, Messiah ben David.

Not even the bit of the iron sword that severs the wall of his crypt. The boy's eyes clear as his assailants flee through the rift in the rock. His hand still upon his pants leg, clutching the belt loop, he does not search for underwear, but drawing on trousers squeezes into his shoes and puts a foot through the wooden barrier. The rent is large enough to squeeze out.

Ostropol tiptoes along the face of the cliff, finds handholds, footholds, scales the sheer rock, like the hind, jumping to a path below.

And now, the Messiah ben David, Simon Ben Kozibah, Kokhaba, son of a star, "The star has trodden forth out of Jacob," touches Maishe with his spark. In the breast of Ostropol, a flame strikes, leaping from the brittle wood of backyard fences, rising from splinters, old rotten balustrades, the slats of tumbledown porches; a fire raged in his small chest bones, crackling across Dorchester. He wishes for his tormentors. He grasps a limb out of the footpath, a cudgel, and breaking it against a tree, swears an oath.

His forehead is hot and his eyes red. Even his mother forbears to ask him about his missing underwear that night; instead washing his woolen skullcap, streaked with blood, shaking her head as the stains flow away in cold, soapy water; while Maishe lies in bed with blazing cheek, speaking among the white sheets to the angels of apocalypse, clutching the neck of chicken feathers in his pillow.

Nose II

Pimples, the Messiah? A leper, untouchable, holy. Sanhedrin 98b, on the suffering Messiah. "The Rabbis said, 'His name is "the leper scholar," as it is written, *Surely he has borne our griefs, and carried our sorrows, yet did we esteem him a leper, smitten of God and afflicted* (Isaiah 53:4).' " There are two Messiahs—Messiah ben David and Messiah ben Joseph. The nations confused one with two, confounded the creature of melancholy with the bright hero of the End of Days.

Joseph, the sad comedian.

"Melancholy is not a sin, but it dulls the heart more than the gravest sin … After the soul-searching that comes from melancholy, a man goes to sleep, being unable to bear himself, much less his friend, and seething with anger. But after the soul-searching that comes from bitterness, a man cannot sleep. For what actually is bitterness? The recognition that you have not begun to do good deeds ... Now you are a Jew ... Nevertheless, you must know that only a hair's breadth separates bitterness from melancholy." Reb Aaron of Pinsk warns, "There are some young scholars who think they are bitter, when in fact they are simply melancholy."

"Scratch, tear," as the doctor says, rend yourself in two, *Sorrow is better than laughter: for by sadness of countenance the heart is made better* (Ecclesiastes 7:3).

Skin Before Skin

"**Mrs. Ostropol, I'm glad to report, 99.9 percent** in tip-top physical health, fourteen years old, ready for the Marines, really 100 percent, nothing wrong. Listen—nothing wrong."

"Why?"

"Why? Dear mother, why not? He's changing, an adolescent, no longer your little *tchahtchkee*. He's becoming a man, so, some things are growing fast, others slow, who knows?"

"All day in bed, Mrs. Ostropol?"

"Maybe he's depressed, puppy love, he's discovered his *petzelle*."

"All night in the bathroom?"

"Pimples—yes. Why not? I warned him. He's making worse. 'At twenty you'll be Scarface.' Between you and me, normal. Not what he's doing now, you're right, lacerating. subcuticle surgery. He's making something out of nothing. Interesting. Psychopathic? Take him to a psychiatrist? A waste! Your son wants something to be wrong. Why scratch so hard? I've seen dozens like this. Let him—encourage it, rip, tear, pluck. Come out of the bathroom, face bleeding, in bandages, soaking up lotions, white ointments, a walking mummy, a film of gauze, adhesive, clay, wrapped around him. Normal, Mrs. Ostropol, half of teenage Dorchester walks around this way. Normal? It's exaggeration, Mrs. Ostropol! A few white heads, one or two pustules, a sprinkling across the nose is not enough. More. They want more, theatrical horrors. Your son, one of worst, is a hypermanic renderer of the flesh. To what end? All flesh is grass. It's normal. Out Mrs. Ostropol, out! Next, next please, next."

• • •

"Margy, who is that boy with the bandage on his right cheek and chin?"

"You know him, Sandy, that smart ass from Dorchester. He's not even premed but what a pain with the books, did you read *this*, *that*? All the time like a walking library."

"Oh Jesus, he saw us looking at him, *Margy!*"

"Look, he's squeezing his *cheek*, Sandy. He must think he has a dimple."

(Laughter)

"He's getting up, *Margy!*"

"Oy vey. Quick. Look the other way, oh that cute Danny Kaplan …"

"Margy, did you *really* find that adorable blouse in *Filene's*?"

"I was just rummaging with Mommy and … My God!"

" … "

"Hi. *Margy* and what?"

"Hi. And I put my hand in …"

" … "

"I'm Sandy."

"We met *you* already." (Laughter) "And Sandy … *Try* to remember, since you're *so* smart."

"Sandy Berger."

"And I'm the Queen of Sheba."

"Not dark enough?"

"How do *you* know?"

"Margy's from Miami Beach."

(Giggles.) "What happened to *your* face?"

"A leper?" (Giggles.)

"Help. *Margy*, help!"

"Get away, get away. *Danny*, is this *your* friend?"

"Des-who?"

"Who says *you* exist?"

"So *stop* thinking, Mr. Descartes."

"So *Sandy*, how did your mother get her *hands* on the *blouse*?"

"Margy, there was this other lady …"

"Please, tell it to my *mother*."

"What?"

"*Margy?*"

"*Sandy!*"

"*Margy*, I heard about this. *Danny*, Danny! Get my *mother?*"

"You shouldn't talk about God."

"I'm going to call her *down* here. I'm *going* to …"
"She doesn't have to …"
"He doesn't *have* to strike you *dead*."
"By a count of ten, doesn't prove …"
"*Momma!*"
"Don't *count* …"
"*Momma!*"

• • •

"Did you ever …"
"Once … almost."
"Why?"
"You wanna try?"
"I …"
"Mmmmmmm."
"No."
"Mmmmmmm."
"No … oh …"

• • •

"Seven weeks."
"It's not *my* fault."
"My period.
"I didn't get it."
"You know we *could* get married."
"Why don't we get *married*?"
"Mmmmm …"
"Mmmmmm …"

• • •

"It was a false …"

"We can still …"

"My mother made arrangements. My *mother*. What am I going to tell her, and the *Rabbi*. And I love you."

"I love you. *Maishe* doesn't that mean *anything*?"

"You didn't have fun?"

"We sent out *invitations*."

"But you, I thought you *loved* …"

"You're so cute, when you do *that* …"

"When you pout and your eyes cross. Every time you get excited and you blink, did you *know* that? Watch, look in the mirror … And the Rabbi, *Maishee*, what could I say to the *Rabbi*?"

• • •

"So you are the lucky young man …"

"Harvard, very nice …"

"I'd like to have a few words before …"

"A spiritual understanding."

"Harvard, myself …"

"Yes, but you *like* her?"

"Doubts …"

"Harvard …"

"Yourself …you can't …"

"If you look at it …"

"Not as a certainty, but a possibility …"

"Judaism doesn't ask any more than a possibility …"

"A straw …"

"Me too."

"Miserable."

"Straw."
"Straw."
"Straw."
"Straw."

HERE'S CHAIM CHOKKING!

Jew of the Week—who will it be? Not me—this time. Instead, out of Feinberg's Five and Dime—can the Feinbergs be proud? Let's hear it for, *loud*, Rabbi Moses Ostropol Spiritual Guide of Newton's Most Modern Temple, Beth Oh-hav-toh Harvard College Graduate, Roxbury teacher, Des Moines Iowa, American Rabbinical Seminary. Happy to Have You Home! Crime for a Dime! Feinbergs Celebrates, A Sale on Dry Goods, Piece of the World to Come, Two for One, prices are out of this world.

Gottenyu! WHAT MORE CAN THEY DO?

Nose III

Odors stream in spirals from the text: myrrh, cloves, cherry cough medicine.

How shall we know Messiah?

Ask not, how shall we know him. Ask, how shall *he* know us?

Discussing the advent of Messiah, the Annointed One, his hair wet with oil, the Talmud, (Sanhedrin 94a) quotes the cryptic lines of Isaiah (21:11). *The burden of Dumah. He calls to me out of Seir. "Watchman, what of the night? Watchman, what of the night?"'* Rabbi Jonathan explains: "The angel in charge of spirits is called Dumah. All the spirits come before Dumah to ask when redemption, or 'morning' will come, and when the exile, or 'night' will end. They cry, 'What says the watchman of the night? What says the watchman of the night?' And the watchman answers them *"The morning comes, and also the night, if he will inquire, inquire, ye, return, come"* (Isaiah 21:12).

Redemption from the first exile is coming, but alas, a second exile awaits us. "*Return*," the watchman cries, meaning, "Repent!" The sage Rashi tolls the watchman's bell coming closer and closer—"Redemption comes for the righteous as 'morning' but also the 'night,' punishment for the wicked."

How shall he, the Messiah, know us, the righteous from the wicked?

He shall smell us out. That is "good divinity …To say 'ay' and 'no' to every thing." But how do the rabbis derive this? They return to Isaiah (Sanhedrin 93b). "The Messiah—as it is written. *And the spirit of the Lord shall rest upon him, the spirit of wisdom and understanding, the spirit of counsel, and might, the spirit of knowledge of the fear of the Lord. And shall make him of quick understanding in the fear of the Lord*" (Isaiah 11:2).

Here the rabbis begin to laugh. (Don't they care for the Messiah?) Rabbi Alexandri says, "Look at the poor Messiah. He is staggering—such a load. Look at all the things that are '*resting*' on him: '*counsel*,' '*might*' '*wisdom*,' '*fear*.' "

At his ear, the sage, Raba, puns on the similarity between the noun for "quick understanding, *hariycho*, that for resting—*rachayiim*," and the verb "smells, *rayach*." Raba cries, "He smells a man and judges, as it is written *and he shall not judge after the sight of his eyes, neither*

45

reprove after the hearing of his ears, yet with righteousness shall he judge the poor."

(How does Raba, sage of Babylon, derive his reading? Is it far-fetched? Hardly. Rather it is the standard interpretation of Isaiah *and he shall be of quick understanding, [wa-haricho]* which employs a metaphoric usage of the Hebrew [*hoh-rayach*] from which it derives means to smell. (See Leviticus 26:31), *And I will not smell [ohriyach] the savor of your sweet odors,*" and check Exodus 30:38. "*Whosoever shall make like unto that, to smell [horiyach] thereof, he shall be cut off from his people.*" How it came about that smell and quick understanding were associated can be seen in the usage of the word in Job 39:25: "*He saith among the trumpets, ha, ha, and he smelleth [yoriyach] the battle from afar off.*" If the horse smells battle from afar, he understands before anyone else what is happening.) Even more telling is the passage in which it occurs, for the Hebrew sets up an evident pun by its very repetition of the word, *ruach*, spirit, which is the ancient root of *riyach* or smell. Edward Horowitz, "Coming from *ruach*, wind, is *rayach*, odor, meaning a smell or fragrance which is carried by the wind, from *rayach* we have *hariyach*, he smelled."

Isaiah 11:1-4, the source of so much speculation on the Messiah, reads: *And a shoot shall sprout out of the stock of Jesse and a stem out of his roots. And it shall rest upon him—Spirit of*

God, spirit of wisdom and understanding, spirit of counsel and might, spirit of knowledge and of fear of God. And he shall be in-spirit-ed [hariy-cho—of quick understanding] in the fear of God. And not by the sight of his eyes, shall he judge, and not by what his ears hear, shall he chastise. But with righteousness shall he judge the poor and chastise with equity for the poor of the earth: and he shall strike the earth with the rod of his mouth, and with the spirit of his lips shall he slay the wicked.

If he doesn't use his *eyes* and doesn't use his *ears*, how will the Messiah judge?

He smells. He is a creature of smell, the same root in Hebrew as spirit, breath.

(Since smell and spirit are so close, see that the Messiah judges not from external evidence but from the very internal essence of a man. He can smell guilt, fear. Is this the importance of smell, incense, to the Holy One? Smell directs our judgment. In the words of Exodus 5:21, when the children of Israel complained about being brought into ill repute with Pharaoh, "*You caused our smell to stink in the eyes,*" the very definition of the fear of judgment, to be in bad odor.)

From the Talmud, Sanhedrin 93b, "Bar Kokhba reigned two and a half years and then said to the rabbis, 'I am the Messiah.'

"They answered, 'Of Messiah it is written that he smells and judges, let us see whether he,

Bar Kozibah can do so.' When they saw that he was unable to judge by smell, they slew him."

This is embroidered on further in the Zohar and Yalkut Reubeni. When Isaac was tied to the altar for the sacrifice, it was too terrible for him to endure in his own body on the earth. His soul went up to heaven, as it is written, "etherealized …he ascended to the throne of God like the odor of the incense of spices which the priests offered before Him twice a day." (Zohar 120a). The angels drew Isaac up to Heaven and when the horror was over, brought him down. But he had the smell of the Garden and Eden sticking to him. That's where they took him while Abraham raised his knife over the bones below. Whether Isaac went up to Eden or no, he was a sweet savor in the nose of the Holy One. He smelled delicious. So Messiah (who has been waiting in the Garden for four thousand years to come down, living in perfumes of good) can *smell* a bad deed.

Which Messiah? Messiah ben Joseph, Messiah ben David? The rabbis knew about the *other*, who takes a fall, the failed Messiah. He has to come first.

It's the leper carrying grief, woe, trouble, counsel, understanding, *smitten of God and afflicted* (Isaiah 53:4), the world on his shoulders. A man who won't break *a bruised reed* but still goes into battle in the middle of the nightmare of the Great Judgement.

Why should Joseph come first?

He gives a lesson to the next one, his successor, Messiah ben David. Sukkah 52a, "The Holy One, blessed be He, will say to the Messiah, the son of David (May he reveal himself speedily in our days) 'Ask me anything, I will give it to you,' as it is said, *I will publish the decree, God said to me, you are my son, for this day have I begotten you, ask me and I will give the nations for your inheritance.*' (Psalms 2:7-8) But when he [the Messiah ben David] will see that the Messiah, the son of Joseph is slain, he will say to Him, 'Lord of the Universe, I ask of You only the gift of life.' "

Messiah ben David arrives in trepidation. Sanhedrin 97a: "In the generation when the son of David will come, scholars will be few in number, and as for the rest, their eyes will fail through sorrow and grief. Multitudes of trouble and evil decrees will be promulgated anew, each new horror will run to there before the other one is over."

Call the roll! (Sanhedrin, 97a-99a.)

Rabbi Judah? "In the generation when the son of David comes, the Academy will be for whores. Galilee in ruins, Gablan desolate, the border dwellers wander from city to city receiving no welcome, the wisdom of scribes in disfavor, God-fearing men despised, people be dog-faced and truth entirely lacking, as it is written, *Yea truth faileth and he that departeth from evil maketh himself a prey* (Isaiah 49: 15)."

Rabbi Nehorai? "In the generation when Messiah comes, young men will insult old, and old men will stand before young [to honor them]: daughters will rise up against their mothers, and daughters-in-law against their mothers-in-law. The people shall be dog-faced, and a son will not be abashed in his father's presence."

Rabbi Nehemiah? "In the generation of Messiah's coming, impudence will increase, esteem be perverted, the vine yield its fruit, yet wine be costly and the Kingdom shall convert to heresy with no one to rebuke them."

Rabbi Isaac? "The son of David will not come until the whole world is converted to the belief of heretics."

Rabbi Johanan, "The son of David will come only in a generation which is all righteous or all wicked."

Rabbi Jose b. Kisma, "Place my coffin deep in the ground, for there is not one palm tree in Babylon to which a Persian horse will not be tethered, nor one coffin in Palestine out of which a Median horse will not eat straw."

Rabbi Ulla? "Let Messiah come, but let me not see him."

Rabbi Rabbah? "Let him come, but let me not see him."

Birth pangs—labor cramps—Messiah is coming out and every man gives birth to him, as it is written: *Ask now, and see whether a man labors with a child? Why do I see every man with his hand on his loins like a woman in labor and all faces are turned pale?* (Jeremiah 30:6). A thousand years of horror. As Rabbi Johanan says, "When you see a generation ever dwindling, hope for him, as it says, *And the afflicted people will You save.* (Samuel II 22:28). When you see a generation overwhelmed by many troubles as a river, await him. *When the enemy shall come in like a flood, the Spirit of the Lord shall lift up a standard against him. And the Redeemer shall come to Zion.*" (Isaiah 59:19-20.)

A thousand years? A thousand years of pregnancy? There are still crueler prophecies. Rabbi Hillel?

"Why even ask? For Israel there will be no Messiah. They already ate their fill of him, enjoyed, during the reign of Hezekiah."

Rabbi Giddal in the name of Rab objects. "We Jews *will* eat our fill in the days of Messiah."

They raise their voices, their arms, pushing for places at the banquet table. It has come to sticks and stones before in the schoolhouse. But the melancholic whisper of Rabbi Zera interrupts them. "Why think about it? Whenever you count, you postpone it. He would have come already, if the scholars had not tried to set a date. For it was taught, 'Three things come without warning, Messiah, what's lost then found, and a scorpion.'"

L'CHAIM DE CHAIM

So it's bon voyage and *l'chaim*,
tears and happy waves from all
of Newton, Brookline, and Brighton.
Thanks to Goebell's Travel Agents
200 luck, luck, lucky ladies
off with Rabbi Moses Ostropol
on the Grand Jewish Tour:
Amsterdam, Toledo, Tangiers
Holy Land Awaits You! *Mazel
Tov* from Everyone left behind!

The Doctor

After the catastrophe, after the blow which came down on their heads as if all the windows in the John Hancock building had buckled at once, leaving them staring at a shattered image; the best doctor in Boston was called in to address the congregation, en masse, in a special-after-the-service-chat. Chochom Kezzlev (psychiatrist to the mayor, superintendent of schools, the commissioner of mental health, the governor, cardinal, wife of the grand rabbi, the grand rabbi's children, wizards of the financial district), spoke to the membership for four hundred dollars a head, the fee would be attached to the bill for their seats at Rosh Hashanah, to make for them what was announced in the pages of the temple bulletin as a "psycho-sermon-ette /analysis," attendance mandatory but deductible on Blue Cross/Blue Shield.

"This is classical," Chochom whistled through his front teeth at Beth Ohavtoh, laying the *Schokolade mit Schlagsahne*, Vienna *uber* Roxbury on, to soothe the ladies, gentlemen, rocking back and forth, crying, why, why, their baby, their rabbi?

"Schizophrenia!" He banged the pulpit like his father, an official of the Ironmongers' Shul on Blue Hill Ave. "Schizophrenia," he hammered (until everyone quieted down). "Schizophrenia … schizophrenia … schizophrenia."

"Tonight," he whispered in the stillness as the last cough died away, whipping his chocolate vowels, "Is not a night to be technical.

"Split.

"He split.

"The young man split in two.

"You thought you had one rabbi, but really there were two. A daily double. Two for the price of one. I'm making fun. Only let's be serious.

"Maishe Ostropol 'one' is a nice young man, personable, amiable, intelligent, well spoken, easy to know, generous, available to friends, attentive to strangers, open to the whole community; fund-raiser, speaker, chairman of a dozen committees, good husband, loving son-in-law. Fill in the boxes, superior, excellent, 100 percent, to lapse into dialect, a *mensch*.

"Ostropol 'two' is secretive, unfriendly, nervous, irritable, ugly, subject to depression, one day up, next day down, can't sit still, jumps around, runs out a back door half naked, grabs you by coat lapels, cries, then kisses, blesses. He wants to know personal details, your deals, sex practices, spouts about wife swapping ritual murder, let's try to open up, fresh breezes in the temple, *ruach, ruach*, new spirit through the synagogue doors, blow, blow—remember that sermon?

"You do? Me too. I didn't attend but patients called in to cancel appointments. I knew something was up. Is this the young man I met at the Jewish Charities Purim Ball who talked Freud, Jung, Adler, Erickson at me, after a benediction even the Viennese doctor could have said a hearty *ohmayn* to?

"I sent him a card. 'Come in—free consultation!' What do I get back? An unsigned note; the local police laboratory traced it back to a typewriter in your temple. The card disparaged the medical profession, with scurrilous quotes out of context from sources in antiquity. I'm not complaining! I want you to know that this isn't the first time your rabbi's case crossed my desk. For years, I have been taking notes, expecting a break? Why? When a man so respected, influential in the community, cracks, the community cracks? You have mass hysteria. I've got case histories on half of Boston and its suburbs. You know the city. It can blow, blow. Keep an eye on crackpots!

"I put my finger in the crack. I don't want to get personal. I know the family is here, a wife, a mother-in-law, friends of his domestic circle, I'm not going to talk sex. Biography! A confused boy, shaky adolescence, early marriage, out of nowhere a rabbinical career?

"In the community, on the bema, a leader. Your building fund doubled, your youth group tripled, glad-handing, smiling, a student who barely passes through *chedar*, suddenly Hebrew trips on his lips, pouring oil on the troubled waters. Respected by

Conservatives, Orthodox, yet at home, troubled, troubled. What is he doing at the Shebbibah Rebbe's house, singing, dancing, drinking until four in the morning? How about the Israeli *hora* contest in the red light district on Columbus Ave, special invitation only? Half of Boston's prostitutes show up, screaming whoopee. When the police burst in Ostropol and the Shebbibah are in a back room giving prizes. Claim they are looking for the Queen of Sheba. That didn't get in the newspapers. Or that the Shebbibah Rebbe is a Yemenite runaway from a Brooklyn insane asylum, his ordination from a Philadelphia yeshiva for draft dodgers. The Shebbibah who tried to horn in on the collection racket in Roxbury with Chassidic strongmen, Hungarians deported from Israel, and ran the short-lived Hebrew Terrorist League. This from Rabbi Moses Ostropol who titillated Brookline with *Bring Home Ham for Passover*, gave at Hancock Hall a lecture, "God is dead, so take His Place," astounded a businessman's luncheon with *Laban and Labor Value*? Running here, there, covering the bases. The patter begins to assert itself, familiar, frightening, out-of-the-dark Hebrew ...

"*Oy kindeh*! A good boy, a bad boy. A Doctor Jekyll, a Mr. You Know Who. I spent months reading up, consulting, not just medical reports, neurological charts, electroencephalograms, but I telegraphed to Jerusalem, the top man in this, esoteric and metaphysical hysteria, a gentleman with degrees from Berlin, Zurich, the Sorbonne, a linguist in thirty languages, Mandarin Chinese, Yiddish, Akkadian, Old Turkic, a master of papyrus scraps, steppe dialects, with the largest collection of data on this problem in his own library and after three weeks of exhaustive research, double, triple checking, verifying the reports I had you all fill out, details I gathered in our preliminary interviews, midnight meetings, consultations on sexual problems, reading lists, the trip itself, and I want to ask how that trip took place, how two hundred of you out there, husbands, respectable middle-class businessmen, lawyers, doctors, could have trusted this young man; and it's a testimony to his magnetism, his *brillé*, that you willingly, without a whisper, allowed your wives to fly off in the custody of a healthy, youthful male not bringing his own mate along. All those girls (you'll pardon me, ladies, at my age, but you are so fresh, blooming, that to me you'll be forever *girls*) not unchaperoned but only too chaperoned, and you didn't recognize, you didn't see, what's clear to me, am I a scholar, the son of a scholar? Who do you think *he* was? "It's him!" the telegram said from Jerusalem. "Him!" You're in trouble. You didn't know. *Gornisht mit gornisht*! Hyde! Hyde! Your rabbi thought, only worse, better. A glass of water, please! 'It's Him.' Water!

"*Gottenyu*! God is sick. You didn't know that. Before you begin with the 'God is dead' business, you got to have God sick. An old story—you didn't hear out in Newton, at the country club, the swimming pool. You forgot what your parents, grandparents knew. An old story among Jews. We're sick, so God is sick. The sicker we are, the sicker He is. We're sicking with Him.

"Sick, sick, sick. The rabbis found out about this. Kaballah, secret knowledge, eh, scared? Good! As God goes under, He does a lot of damage. It's not me who's talking. Don't blame me. Did I attend Him? For years, however, some of the greatest rabbis have had God under examination, on the table. You think Freud was the first psychiatrist? Please. Ever hear of Rabbi Isaac Luria, the Lion? In the sixteenth century already, they knew, God had a breakdown, a split. 'It's Him, it's Him.' What's this, a House of Study or a country club? You came to find out something ha? That's what the rabbi had on his mind.

"Sickness.

"The sicker you are, the closer to God, how's that? Don't let God die—too late—it's all over. Trash, all those lectures of Ostropol! I've been through his notes. I know what was on his mind. God is dead was a masquerade. No one but eggheads, empty shells, could get any comfort out of that; nothing to suck on but an empty planet. No, God was alive but in hiding, Argentina, Israel, Amsterdam. What are you doing there? Is this a House of Study? Start looking. Get under the seats! Where is He? He's tarrying? Where? Where?

"Only *kindeh* careful. This is not for everyone.

"Some of you knew nothing. Others got hints, side looks, pinches, anonymous letters. In his library, a manual, I found, how to be a heretic, a *marrano*, secret Jew. Button your lip, seem the opposite of what you are, open your mouth only to lie. Do something bad in order to be aware of what is good. You know what this is?

"Deliberate, *gevult a klog*, deliberate, premeditated, schizophrenia. Schizophrenia with forethought. Maishe

Ostropol split but not by accident. He took an axe and cleft himself in two. You know what can happen, if this gets going, everyone operating on themselves. It's incendiary. Better give out needles and heroin. The Friday Night Special! Only why? Why does he crave a split, a crack, a sieve? In his head he is between good and evil."

"What evil?" cried a voice from the audience.

"We loved him," burst from another.

"You *kuck*!" called Kezzlev. "It's your fault. You loved him. You made him sick. He couldn't handle it. He began to get doubts, questions, riddles, paradoxes, until all he could do in the face of your affection was split, two, a goody, a baddy, Maishe, the Almighty, what's going on? Who knows One? Who knows Two?

"*Meshuggeh mit* Messiah. An old disease, a Jewish ailment. Momma, Momma, you made us crazy.

"Who wants to become the Messiah?"

"God forbid!" a voice wailed.

"Absolutely. God forbid it. He doesn't need competition. He's already sick, think He needs more of it? Leave Him alone. Leave God alone. I don't talk with Him. I'm not claiming anything. Only as a doctor, I'll testify. Anyone who's as sick as He is ought to get some rest. He doesn't need a whole people banging on the door, trying to get into bed with Him. Seven gates, eight gates, you think that kept out the mystics, Rabbi Akiba, Ben Zoma, Abuyah, Ben Azzai, pushing, shoving, to get in to see Him.

"So this is what happened: the rabbi put two and two together and got one. He was sick. God was sick. So, maybe …"

"God forbid," a voice screamed.

"That's what I say. You didn't come here to worship the rabbi. Back! Back on firm ground. Only we aren't in regular medicine. This is old but new, like psychiatry, *nu*, for years people were ill, but the diagnosis wasn't clear. Now, children, for years I studied the problem with Berlin, Jerusalem, Buenos Aires. I conferred, exchanged data, documentation, all the detritus, decades, and we're about to announce, for you an advance preview, a new branch of medicine, special for cases like the rabbi: 'Metasicknix,' diseases of the spheres.

"The rabbi was ill, extraterrestrial. This isn't a simple case. You know, Momma doesn't love him, Daddy was a *shmuck*. That's peanuts, dime a dozen, I can cure, two *grosz* an hour. This Mr. Ostropol wanted to be at the center of the universe, planet, stars, kit and caboodle. The traumas of Jupiter, Uranus, are what he's after. Shock therapy? Talk to me of explosions in the Milky Way. Supernal waters. Amnesia of the Black Hole.

"You got to have tools to lever constellations to doctor in that crack. *Kindeh*! A new science, new tools, tonight, Metasicknix.

"Phenomena in this case defy explanation. Two hundred ladies in this room went on a trip. Where? They can't talk about it. Tel Aviv, Amsterdam? Toledo? No one knows. I got reports from all the major cities on the itinerary. Only what happened is still not clear. Did they go or not? Everyone saw them off. Logan Airport?

I got a bill for 639 glatt kosher corned beef sandwiches with a pickle tucked in, courtesy of Feinberg's caterers. More, no one is positive. El Al isn't talking. His correspondents all tell a tale yet share a common illusion. What's going on? The police are in a state of nervous collapse. Another doctor ... Not me. Certainty, no, but I got Metasicknix.

"Later in the temple bulletin, you'll read more, two hundred depositions, no one tells the same thing. No souvenirs, ticket stubs. Mass amnesia, unstamped passports: two hundred ladies went to sleep for a three-week holiday special. The rabbi did not appear back in the International Arrival Hall on the stroke of seven o'clock Eastern Daylight Savings Time when the rest of the tour woke up in the arms of husbands, relatives, friends, how was it? How was it? "How was it? How was it?" While a frantic *rebbitzin* was screaming louder and louder abetted by a chorus of mother-in-laws, *shammus*, the president, chairman of the brotherhood and representatives of the travel agency: 'Maishe? Maishe?'

"Call for the paddy wagon! Ambulance. Call for the cops? A doctor?

"Call for Philip Morris! Rashi! Ibn Ezra! In the margins, a hint, what became of Maishe, what happened, how was it, with the ladies? Moses de Leon, Nahum of Gaza, the old geographers.

"*Kindeh*, what do I know? You came to me on the hush, hush in a rush, rush.

"Back, to the facts. Schizophrenia. Before we get mixed up with *mishigass*, let's stick with sickness. As long as the rabbi was mixed up, *meshuggeh*, first one, then the other, one night a sweetheart, the next, insane, a demon: everything was all right. Harmless. You are on solid ground. Only one evening, observe, a change. The rabbi's face starts to glow, little sparks around his ears and nose, a crackling in the air as he speaks, and a smile. It melts the heart, an odor goes forth from the pulpit, spices, frankincense, cinnamon, and clove. At the very moment when everyone was yelling, fed up, enough of this baloney, forces underfoot to push him out of the spiritual leadership of Beth Ohavtoh, the president, chairman of the brotherhood, *shammus*, have all come by on their own to confess, ashamed: claiming, they were out of their heads, voices whispering in their ears. Now all this conspiracy is forgotten. The whole *shul*, even the back aisles where the scoffers sit, can't control itself. A word, two, they are crying. All those dead lines in the service are suddenly on their lips. A well of holiness spills out of their throats, the well that Abraham dug, Isaac, the sweet water that Jacob found. A flood, it's rising, rising. Forgive us, forgive us! We're turning, turning.

"Oh, you remember. And it kept on. Week after week. No one could stay away from the synagogue. His smile was driving you crazy. Everything was forgiven, forgiven. Anything seemed possible. Two hundred ladies dreamed of going to the Holy Land and dancing for the sons of Jacob before Mount Zion. Why not? A fabulous group rate. It broke your heart. Everyone wanted to go. Want to go? Go! He's going, we're going too! Just hold on to the fringe of his smile.

"A smile that bore you off to Logan Airport, singing, eyes wet, laughing, carrying Torah scrolls, dancing, until the plane was going in circles. The rabbi with arms lifted up in the middle of his circle of girls whirling round and round, faster and faster in a swirl toward the ramp, beaming, beaming on you. Happy! See? Happy! Happy!

"Ha! Ha! Ha!

"I have seen that smile, oh my children, at the Boston State, Mass Psychopathic, not to disparage, not to make light, I witnessed only a glimmer of what shone forth full flood in Maishe Ostropol, but I'll tell you when the glint strikes through the crack, I start with, lock him up! Lock up the knives, hide the ropes, take away silverware, get cotton batting, mattresses, pad him, her, wrap him up, up, up good.

"Schizophrenia and the razor blade. The smile before the split. He could have led you across the Red Sea smiling, the Charles, the Mystic, dry land in the middle of the waters.

"All the while another half of him is gathering in the nether parts; his head full of goodness, but his bowels swelling, all the evil puffing, ready to explode at the second of his takeoff—pop! Everyone in a cloud of smoke—disappears.

"You know your *Arabian Nights*. Metasicknix. How do I get the rabbi back? A special technique—radical psychosurgery. Operative procedure—soul puncture—an ancient ritual, 100 percent kosher, certified through the centuries. Excommunication!

"We are going to put the *chayriim*, the rabbinical ban on half of Maishe Ostropol. We will drive the evil side out of the community, while grabbing the good side and pulling it back in, simultaneously. However, as this is no normal excommunication but one which involves the substance of the universe which according to Luria, Yitzchock, the Leo, and his disciples, is engaged in a process of refining itself, separating good and evil, holiness and draff, we run risks.

"Imagine, congregants, a tiny atom, so infinitesimal you can't begin to see it and yet a split, a crack—boom! Half the world can fly apart. So, in trying to make a final disposition of the wickedness of Maishe Ostropol, in rearranging the neutrons, we may touch the anatomy of matter, the first Adam, whose corpus makes up our Milky Way. Oy vey. How badly do you want him back?"

"Back, back!" an echo filled the *shul*, shaking the candelabrum on the bema.

"Excommunication!"

"What for?"

"Self abuse," cried Kezzlev. "Consorting with angels. Dreaming of being, help, a Messiah. Help! Hasten Jason get the basin. Help!" The lights went out. A spotlight shone down on the speaker. "I'm him. Look. I'm tearing my clothes. Get away from me. I'm *traif*. I stink. Not kosher. Look, smell, no baths, washcloths. Pheew! Look the whip. See, I'm giving it to myself. Forty stripes save one. Ouch! Ay! Step on me. Everyone. Run up, step on my head. Help! Help!

"Split. I'm splitting."

A crack sounded through the hall. The sun, a bolt of lightning struck the altar. The velvet hangings started to smoke against the ark holding the scrolls of the Law. Hail and sleet rattled the windows. The building began to tip.

A dazed membership clung to its seats, held tight to the arm rests like raft rails. Electrified, Doctor Kezzlev sailed before them, his tongue stuck out, the tips of his white hair on end, levitated above the bema.

A voice spitting into an empty pot rattled in each head, a bone in an empty skull, "Who's your rabbi?"

"We got a doctor," cried someone. "It's better."

Blood cells, nerve endings, spinal marrow, exploded in eight hundred and twenty two heads. A doctor! *Hak mir nisht keyn tshaynik!*

I know you nincompoop, but you don't know me. Or your Talmud. Abba Gurion of Zadian said on the authority of Abba Guria: *One should not teach his son to be an ass driver, camel driver, wagoner, sailor …* Rabbi Judah said in his name: *Most ass drivers are wicked while most camel drivers are worthy men and most sailors are pious. The worthiest of butchers is Amalek's partner. And the best of doctors goes to Gehenna.* Your ancestors started with anatomy, 613 parts of the body and ended with the mystery of creation. You start with mystery and end with anatomy, a tree of terminology. This doctor will burn in hell. *Gey! Gey!* Let the fire that consumed Korah, eat his bones. *Gey, gey, gey in d'rerd.*

"D … D … Dummies. D … D … Dummies," spoke a voice all too corporal. It burst out of the holy ark whose doors flapped like chicken wings. "D … D … Don't p … p … provoke him."

No fire followed. No lightning. Everyone, however, saw, at once, the rabbi.

"Rabbi! Rabbi!" A din filled the temple. The lights came on. Kezzlev descended to earth. And in the noise, their spiritual guide vanished against the ceiling.

"It's Him. Him."

Cyclone strikes Newton!

Short Circuit in Synagogue.
Suspended communications.
Doctor caught in debris.

Sparks

Divine sparks are falling all over Boston. On the golden dome of Bullfinch's statehouse, down the needle of the Customs House tower, raining on Savin Hill, Brighton, Rosindale; showers of brilliant banded drops of color drenching the flat tops of Brookline delicatessens, running through the gutters off Mattapan's Wellington Hill, hot, thick and fast. A torrent pours over the square of green between broken shop fronts on Blue Hill Avenue and the car barns of Forest Hills a mile away—Franklin Park. A column of fire crackles in its puddingstones.

A passenger debarks, kneels between bus and curb, kissing stone. Behind him the bus driver throws out a broken, black vinyl valise, dimmed by the grime of a freighter's hold, the labels, Grenada, Amsterdam, Haifa, Buenos Aires.

His dark rabbinical suit is luminescent, outlined in flame. Not for the eyes of pimps (but three children, African American, see this as they dash by the park entrance on their way from school). The bored bus driver is oblivious (although an inebriated Mr. O'Riley, as the doors close, tries to rise, but an intoxicating fume in his nose collapses him back into his seat). A lady with twelve shopping bags, making a sentimental journey to the pigeons by the zoo, however, recognizes the outline of her former neighbor.

"Maishe," she cries, just as the black valise hits him. Even under his bushy beard, at one hundred yards, this lady detects the family Ostropol from Kingsdale Street, whose tenant she has been. She gathers up two closets, five chests of drawers, now stuffed into paper receptacles. Does the rabbi see this matriarch weighed down with the bulk of her former rooms running to embrace him? Agile with the exercises of the Indian subcontinent, he leaps the wall of the park, then the fence of the zoo, leaving the smell of myrrh, cloves, cherry cough medicine and the faintest tickle on the lady's palate of a cream drenched herring, a spark of *schmaltz*, caught in her throat.

North

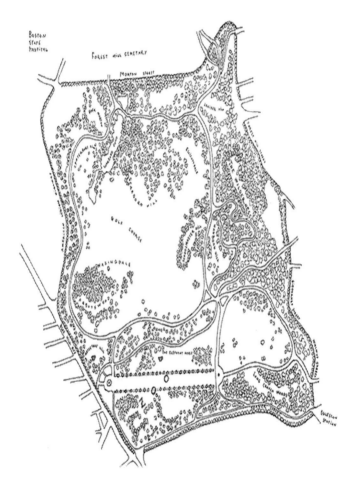

South

Franklin Park

Franklin Park is a quadrilateral, a box, slightly squashed, tilted a bit cockily its corners pointing due north, south, east, and west. One may align it as a green patch of the compass, in the midst of the city of Boston, three miles from the Atlantic. Lower-middle-class streets were built up around it at the turn of the twentieth century. Once Jewish and Irish, now it belongs to Blacks and Hispanics. The park report of 1909 describes "its sides nearly equal in length with minor irregularities and curves. Two of its angles, those to the north and south are somewhat more acute than the others, but are rounded at their points."

The north point jabs Egleston Square—in the late sixties, no-man's-land, struggling Irish, Italians, Blacks. The south pricks the bosom of the State Insane Asylum in Mattapan. "The land extends in its greatest length—one and three-eighths miles, in its greatest breadth one and one-eighth miles, and in its area somewhat more than five hundred acres."

A square mile, but in this book the mile spins; spilling animals, trees, rocks, all falling out.

Put your hand down upon it. Feel.

"Its topography is diversified but not striking, the ground for the most part undulating smoothly. The principal hills and other high places are disposed around and near the borders."

If you grope with your fingers northwest, you feel the knobs of puddingstone. "The western edge abounds in boldly outcropping ledges of conglomerate, falling abruptly in some places fifty or sixty feet. The ridge along the northwestern border is underlain by ledges with numerous outcrops through the thin soil. The highest of these rises to 196 feet above sea level, the greatest elevation in the park." Between the hills, Scarboro, Schoolmaster's, Hagborne and the knolls of Abbotswood, Long Crouch Woods, are the dales and valleys, Nazingdale in the east, Ellicotdale in the "secluded west."

At the southern and eastern corners, the park reaches its extreme depth, forty-eight and thirty-four feet above sea level. This part of Roxbury was known from the eighteenth century as "Canterbury." It was a place of myth, a Canaan to the English colonists in which a tribe of Anakim, a generation of tall demigods, had lived. Ralph Waldo Emerson alludes to them. His friend, Oliver Wendell Holmes retold the legend of a giant embedded in the conglomerate cliffs. If the head of the stone warrior came to the level of the topmost peak, while his feet rested in the cavity of its lowest bog, the great man would measure 244 feet from scalp to toe. In the middle of the twentieth century he could sit on the sixty-foot cliffs along Sigourney, Walnut Street, facing Jamaica Plain, staring towards Newton, West Roxbury, where the Jews are fleeing.

A stone's throw from its northern point, in the squalid square of the same name, dark in the shadows of the elevated trains, is Egleston Station. Walking there, you might have felt the cold December wind blowing the open ends of the wooden platform, its copper ornamentation flaking in wintry green. No matter how your bladder itched in through the 1960s, '70s, the toilet was bolted shut. You might stamp for an hour on the asphalt and cobbles downstairs waiting for the ghost of a trolley—its silver tracks rising out of the tar to crank you down Columbus Avenue until it became Seaver Street. This is the northeast side of the quadrilateral, opposite elegant Roxbury. There are mansions moldering and the bleak ruin of the Mishkan Tefilla Temple, the great house of wealthy, assimilated Jews through the first half of the century. The neighborhood goes to sleep to the howling of animals inside the zoo built here, lions, elephants, a hippo penned into a space not much larger than a bathtub, dying. The grass has long since strangled the Killarneys in Mayor Curley's rose garden.

Skirt the eastern corner, Roxbury is now at your back and fastening on skates, down the slope of Blue Hill Avenue you roller coast past Jewish Dorchester turned to charcoal through the 1970s, movie houses, Franklin, Liberty, shuttered: shops burned out.

Leaving the avenue, skating southwest still on a downward slope you speed past the Hecht House, once a Jewish community center, now abandoned, shut up as surely as the mellahs of Morocco. At the end of American Legion Highway's border with the park, a stream green with water drips from a sewer pipe. This is as far south as the park goes, "low boggy sloughs, only fit for the raising of cabbages." Across the way lay the twisted iron bars and the broad meadows of the State Insane Asylum.

By the madhouse grounds, turn north again. Face a complimentary stretch of green, cemetery lands. Going on straight you would have bumped into buses, elevated trolley lines, the yards of the Metropolitan Transit Authority and a tangle of concrete traffic arteries which have broken up the dream of the park's designer, Frederick Olmsted, for an uninterrupted circle of green through and around Boston. But going around this the corner north yet again, along the western edge, across from horse stables, a stone fence hugs the park. Put your cheek against seam-faced Quincy granite, brush the "grapes, bitter sweet Virginia creepers," that "beneath a canopy of shrubs will cover the walls." Glen Road, Sigourney Street, Walnut Avenue, one jutting, looping into another, skirt this secret part of the park, the Wilderness, Olmsted's concession to Thoreau. "Maple, oak, beech, ash and linden predominate among the trees, while the shrubs consist largely of cornels, thorns, viburnums, Judas trees, sumacs and witch hazels."

The Wilderness arrests attention not for what grows but what once rolled, alive, cold with titanic force—stone. The colonists wrote back to England, struck by the same element, "We found it justly called Roxbury for it was very rocky and hills entirely of rocks."

"The soil is rich and productive … One of its principal features is the conglomerate or puddingstone with which it abounds, much used in church buildings, its brownish hue imparting an air of antiquity to the newest structure …" Geologists tell us that this stone was laid down by glacial action.

The dry remarks about the rock have a bouquet, a residue of myth. "The rounded nodules and plums show the action of water and that the earliest deluge by which the materials of the Roxbury conglomerate were accumulated must have been of great power." Doctor Holmes sang in his poem "The Dorchester Giant" of this glacial slingshot, which resulted in the boulders the English nicknamed, "puddingstone."

> *The suet is hard as a marrow-bone,*
> *And every plum is turned to a stone,*
> *But there the puddings lie.*

The Yankee schoolmaster, Ralph Waldo Emerson, grew up in Franklin Park. The childhood home of the man who came to be known as the "Sage of Concord," sat on a knoll above the meadows. The two companions in middle age Ralph and Oliver walk together, talking to the folds of sheep who used to batten on the grass of Canterbury's meadows. The silver-haired Emerson turns to his genial companion, Holmes, the breakfast table autocrat, intones, "We are always on the brink of an ocean of thought into which we do not yet swim."

He grasps the doctor's arm; "Can you not save me, dip me into ice water, find me some girding belt, that I glide not away into a steam or a gas, and decease in infinite diffusion?"

In the center of a swell, the tidal mass of pudding-stone along the western edge, there is a fragment of foundation. Moses de Leon, contemplating the thir-teenth century mountains of Spain, postulated in his Kabbalah, secret knowledge, "The world did not come into being until God took a certain stone, called the 'Foundation Stone' and cast it into the abyss so that it was held and from that the world was planted … This is the stone referred to in the verses, *Who laid the corner-stone thereof* (Job 38:6), *the stone of testing, the precious corner stone*, (Isaiah 28:16)." Hear the cheru-bim striking their feathers over its chip, implanted in the boulder of conglomerate! So young Ralph Waldo Emerson was moved to testify, in his diary, 1824:

> *Day breaks thro' yonder dusky cloud*
> *O'er well-known cliffs, those giants proud*
> *And I am glad the dame is come*
> *To greet me in my ancient home …*
> *Ye are my home, ye ancient rocks …*

"What are temples & towered cities to him? He has come to a sweeter & more desirable creation. When his eye reaches upwards by the sides of the piled rocks to the grass summit, he feels that the magnificence of man is quelled and subdued here … I stand beneath the same rocks, I touch the same greensward & my heart is exhilarated by the selfsame scenery by which the patriarchs of the infant world pitched their tents, or the herald angels folded their wings when they descended from heaven."

It is the stone on which Jacob rested his head and saw the angels going up and down, pillow and dream. The clouds condense into snow, ice, knit the little rocks together, roll. So the spirit gives form to life even as it melts away in terror, joy.

Spread a picnic down in Nazingdale in the long sloping green of deep clover, dandelions, shorn now to a golf course of velvet nap. Wild blueberries, raspberries, wild roses, rhododendron, bridal wreath, mock orange, under the hemlocks in the ruins of the old Overlook, the Dairy. Through the overturned horn of underbrush run plump raccoons, skunks, woodchuck, squirrel, the white flash of rabbit tail. Pheasant come up in flocks from the tall grass and the fox slinks in its shadows.

Overhead wheel the seasons. Snowy birds settle on the wide green meadows: geese, ducks. Red-winged blackbirds fill the air: crows as large as condors hang like deacons in the bare branches of fall. The dusky sacking of their feathers is a sober attendance on the internment under the snow of blade and leaf. It is winter yet the sky is electric blue. From the brow of hill where Emerson's modest home, a rented farmhouse, stood, even today one cannot see a single housetop but a forest of tree trunks stretching out to the Great Blue

Hill in faraway Canton. Catch breath with the youthful philosopher.

"The air is a cordial of incredible virtue. Crossing a bare common, in snow puddles, at twilight, under a clouded sky, without having in my thoughts any occurrence of special good fortune, I have enjoyed a perfect exhilaration. I am glad to the brink of fear."

Nose IV

The chant from the cooking pots of our fathers' tents: "Come back, little Sheba, come back!"

Sheba's beginning is lost in antiquities, before domestication of the camel or the fall of Ras Shamra. Is Sheba the queen of wisdom or evil, an incarnation of Lilith, a succubus drawn from the skein of divinity? The rabbis forbid the reading of such material to anyone under the age of twenty-nine, thirty-nine. "Sheba. Sheba. Wham bam ba lamba bambalam!"

Holy text itself embodies the contradiction. The earliest references to Sheba sound in a misty past of men and angels, before the waters retreat from the feet of Noah, *Unto Shem also … Elam, and Asshur, and Arpachshad … And Arphachshad begat Shelah: and Shelah begat Eber … And unto Eber … Jokatan … And Jokatan begat … Obal, and Abimael and Sheba.*

And Ophir and Havilah, and Jobab (Genesis 10:21-29).

According to this Sheba is a Semitic patronymic and the Queen is white.

However, even earlier, Genesis 10:6-7, states, *And the sons of Ham, Cush and Mizraim, and Phut and Canaan.* Among *the sons of Cush ... Raama ... and the sons of Raamah: Sheba and Dedan.* Here we find the same Sheba (and his brother, Dedan) as an Ethiopian, a Hamitic patronymic from which we would derive that the queen was black.

Even more confusing, Sheba is a descendent of the patriarch Abraham, Genesis 25:1-3. "*Then again Abraham took a wife, and her name was Keturah. And she bare him Zimran, and Jokashan, and Medan, and Midian, and Ishbak, and Shuah. And Joksham begat Sheba and Dedan ...*"

Is Sheba white, black or caramel, the son of Shem, Cush or Abraham? The curtain drawn— no admission to minors!

In the *Zohar* at the edge of Creation's mysteries there is no color, neither black nor white, red or green at the beginning, but "a shapeless nucleus enclosed in a ring." (Zohar, Bereshith:15a). But suddenly there is brightness. "The Most Mysterious struck its voice and caused this point to shine." It is from the extension of this spot that the universe as light emanates but it is a light unlike any imaginable. As it extended it withdrew—that ebb and flow produced a refuse. These are the questions of chaos and formlessness, "*tohu and bohu*." Darkness beat on the waters, under the lesser and greater lights. It is in this world that Sheba, Lilith, the Covering, were born separate or the same. They are creatures of the fiery darkness, black fire, like the cherubim, the "little faces" (since they have the faces of infants or little children), made of "fire consuming fire."

"After the primordial light was withdrawn there was created a 'membrane for the marrow,' a covering and this covering expanded and produced another. As soon as this second one came forth she went up and down till she reached the cherubim. The covering desired to cleave, to be shaped as one of them. But the Holy One, blessed be He, removed the covering and made her go below." Back and forth, the poor remnant, a film of holiness, wandered until the Holy One, "created Adam and gave him a partner. As soon as the covering saw Eve clinging to his side and was reminded by his form of the beauty above, she flew up from there and tried as before to attach herself to the 'little faces.' " The "little faces" are a tender euphemism for the fruit of nocturnal emission. The same seed that in the darkness of the womb creates palpable children, male and female, outside of it makes the creatures of fantasy. So the covering went back and forth, as a skein of beauty, Lilith, among the shapes of women, Adam and Eve had imagined, children born of seeds spilled in a dream, drops of sweetness in the night. But Lilith does not want her dominion. It is Adam she wants. "The Holy One, blessed be He, scolded and cast her into the depths of the sea where she lived until the moment Adam and his wife sinned. Then the Holy One, blessed be He, drew her from the depths in which she had been confined and gave her power over all those children, the "little faces," that appear in men's semen, creatures liable to punishment for the sins of their fathers …

"When Cain was born this covering tried for a time without success to attach herself to him, but at last she lay with him and bore spirits and demons. Adam for a hundred and thirty years had intercourse with female spirits until Naamah was born. She by her beauty led astray the 'sons of God,' Uzza and Azael, and she bore them children, and so from her went forth evil spirits and demons into the world. She wanders about at night, bedeviling the sons of men and causing them to defile themselves" (Zohar, Bereshith 19b).

The Arabs preserve the tradition that the Queen of Sheba was a sorceress and the daughter of a female *djinn*, devil or genie. The legends of the Jews link Sheba with Lilith, the primal Eve. Ginzberg: "Among the adversaries that assailed him (Job) was the Queen of Sheba. She lived at a great distance from his residence.

It took her and her army three years to travel from her home to his. She fell upon his oxen and his asses and took possession of them, after slaying the men to whose care Job had entrusted them. One man escaped alone." Is this ancient Sheba a primal Eve, who is called Lilith, identical to the covering or *K'fillah*? Was she an ancient consort of the Holy One as a constituent of the undivided light in the days before the Most Mysterious struck its head against the void? In the time of the later patriarchs, she attacks the holy soul, Job. But if the Queen of Sheba is a demon with hairy legs under her skirts as furry as a monkey, did not Solomon, the king, create a hair remover, overlook her flaws in his desire to "know" her. The scholars blush. Ginzberg: "Certain particulars concerning the relations between the Queen of Sheba and Solomon have been omitted here because of their too realistic character." In the Arabic legend in which the queen bears the name *Bilkis* (Hebrew for "concubine") the genii want to hinder the marriage of Solomon and Sheba. They call the king's attention to the growth of hair on her legs. Solomon builds a palace of glass so as not to embarrass his guest by lifting her skirts. But when he looks up he sees—! He mixes up a solution "arsenic and unslaked lime" to remove it.

Why do the genii desire to hinder the marriage of Solomon to one of their own? Sheba is the mother of witches. Solomon is the king of earthly kings. They may go around in the circles of a future paradise. The Queen of Sheba, a demon, is also a bride of Messiah.

In Isaiah, she appears blazing with light, "*Get up, shine, for your light is come and the glory of the Lord rises on you! For look, the darkness shall cover the earth, and gross darkness the people, but the Lord shall rise upon you, and his glory shall be seen upon you. And the nations shall come to your light, and kings to the brightness of your rising … Then shall you see and glow and your heart shall fear and be enlarged … The multitude of camels shall cover you, the dromedaries of Midian and Ephaph: all they from Sheba shall come. They shall bring gold and incense: and bear tidings of the praise of the Lord.*" (Isaiah 60:1-6).

Oh large heart, Sheba, see, smell, glow.

Rabbis

The jaw of Rabbi Akiba sprouted grass at the corner of Seaver Street and Blue Hill Ave., a bleached lower molar rattling every time the trolley came clanging round the corner.

"I … Ish … Ishmael," he stuttered to a piece of cranial cavity, embedded in the ground.

Yes, thought Rabbi Ishmael, I'm listening.

"W … w … what w … w … would you say, if I told you the Queen of Sheba w w … was living in Roxb … b … bury?"

I would think, Ishmael replied, though your is spirit is ascending to the sixth of the seven heavens, through the eyes of Red Adam, the primordial man; on its way through the Sefiroth, and not contradicting a jot of emoluments, praises or glories due to you, Akiba precious oil—you are *f'drayed in the kop*.

"Yet I s … s … smell her, Ishy."

You, my colleague, at whose stutter universes shake upon their pinwheels, who kisses, caresses, adorns with seventy crowns of graven and inscribed letters the Law;

whose word flies to the Holy One, blessed be He, as it traverses seventy thousand worlds till it comes to that throne where He savors, delights, and adds three hundred and seventy thousand crowns; its sound beating out a new sky, new earth, concealed all the while in the shadow of the ancient's armpit for fear of jealous angels, but—Akiba! Despite a molar illuminating all before, casting into dark all behind, you do not possess one infinitesimal *achtel* of smell.

"I t ... t ... taste her."

Where?

"T ... t ... tooth. Against my tooth."

The shred of cranial cavity stirred. The clanging of the Mattapan trolley on its way to Egleston shook Ishmael's repose. How could Akiba receive the sensation of smell through taste? Had the scent of the Queen of Sheba soaked through the subsoil of Franklin Park and tupped a tooth root. What does she taste like?

"S ... s ... sweet."

The perfume of the queen, since it partook of the female presence of the Holy One, had distilled itself into musk. This seeped into the soil between the cracks in the sidewalk through a smoky veil of asphalt to the bottom of potholes, under cobbles, in the ash of backyards as it permeated the earth of Roxbury and was drawn to the remains of the two sages. Mingling with the underwater table it was now nourishing the park. Sweet, yes, but how did Akiba become aware of the sweetness, drop by drop? Did it perhaps wobble the edge of him in a sugary trickle?

"R ... r ... rapt."

How does this taste come to you?

"W … wr … Wrapped."

Wrapped?

"Ha ha haa."

Akiba, it's been almost two thousand years. Act your age!

"Ha … Ha … Ha."

The Queen of Sheba is in Roxbury?

"T … t … tickles."

It is not a wet sensation?

"N … n … no."

Where is the tickling most extreme?

"The t … t … tip."

The tip of the tooth?

"The t … t … tip of the t … t … tickling."

Akiba, the Queen of Sheba—distilled into a dew, fallen on Roxbury, sunk into the soil—has drawn her sweetness up into the body of a root and is now touching you in one green tendril, seeking to entwine your soul.

"W … w … why?"

Ha Ha Ha.

"W … w … what's the matter?"

Me too, she tickled me.

"I … I … Ishy!"

Shah. Ha! Ha! Ha! Hee! Hee!

"It's i … m … m … moral."

Tohu and *bohu*, ever since the Temple fell, everything has been turned upside down, topsy-turvy. That's how we expressed it. Luria baked the whole universe in the shape of his brain, a clay pot that went to pieces in sunlight. The Holy One cooks, but everything must bubble over, until man helps out. Right now, no one is there at the appointed time. Akiba, what are we doing in Franklin Park? You and I should be basking in the sun at Ein Gedi, not getting a chill in icy marrow half the year. As for Sheba, why here? Wasn't she from Ethiopia? You say the queen is in Roxbury? She must have come for us.

"Ishy. You are a w ... w ... well-plastered cistern. You don't lose a d ... d ... drop."

He, Ishmael, was a lump of skull off which the Romans had flayed the skin, bleached like a rock, a relic gathered by a superstitious burial attendant, rattling about in a dusty drawer in Babylon listening to endless restatements of a worm-eaten code, a few good stories; afterwards North Africa, Spain, Ishmael had to keep learning languages.

Meanwhile through the Eye, flying upward, sparks thickening, Ishmael felt the approach of other worlds, presences, the sigh of music that drew him into a single throb; gathered into the skirts of a great female sweetness; on the crosscurrents of so many dreams that he could hardly believe it when in Vilna, cast into the bottom of a bag of dirt from the Holy Land, who bumped into him? A tooth of his old antagonist, Rabbi Akiba, stuttered, "Hello. H ... h ... how do you do? I ... Ish ... Ishmael?"

Akiba? Whose mouth made of the five books of Moses into mayhem, multiplying the law until everyone was bewildered, wandering in a sea of embroidery, every letter turned into a universe of its own! Akiba now short winded, succinct?

"W ... w ... why?"

Why are you stuttering?

"B ... b ... bonehead."

Rabbi Ishmael wondered until his own bone began to tickle.

Zoo

In front of the park gates, tall pillars of marble, white limestone crowned with curled ferns, Corinthian leaves, a woman appears. She is dressed in black silks, wearing a thick fur coat of soft Alaskan seal, dark stockings; her hair, raven, pinstriped with gray. Heavily rouged, the lipstick thick as jam on the Cupid's bow above her teeth, she runs to the right gate, the left, grimacing at the cracked frieze above the entryway, its buffalo, lioness.

She grasps the bars of the central gate, shakes on them.

Three boys, deep purple, brown molasses, light coffee, turn in their stroll across the wide lawn that stretches down to Blue Hill Avenue and stare at her. "*Chazzur!*" she cries, trying to budge the heavy iron posts. A string of white pearls about her neck break and one by one the globules strike the concrete as she stamps her high heels on the pavement.

"*Chazzur!*" She slips, rolls on one pearl like a drunk, almost tumbling, bends down, shrieks.

"You lose something lady?" The boys leap and bound toward the woman on her knees.

"A diamond?" asks T. Booker Lee, the shortest of the three, scratching his shaved head. His two companions space their broad hands over the cracks in the creamy sidewalk. The lady opens her coat, clutches at the string broken open but still hanging from her neck. A few more of the pearls fall as she snatches the strand.

"That what you looking for?" P. Washington Davis, tallest of the boys, cries, trapping six rolling under his quick palm. He scoops them into his other hand and offers them, gleaming to the lady. "Where you putting them?"

Her ghostly fingers shine with crimson lacquer at their tips. P. Washington looks down at the fleck of blood blossoming in his soft palm, where the polished nails jabbed. The woman dumps his offering in a pocket of her fur coat. One pearl, missing the slot, hops on the pavement. T. Booker, bowing, closes his hand around the silver flea. The lady turns back to the iron grate, calls in again, "*Chazzur!*"

"You want to get in?" asks the third boy, Montgomery Richmond, a recent arrival in the Boston area.

P. Washington grasps one of the black tulips in the wrought iron fence, hoists himself in the air. "You like elephants?"

"They got a rhino there," adds Montgomery.

"Bigger than a Cadillac," T. Booker offers.

"Which you like better?" asks Montgomery.

"You want to ride a rhino or a Cadillac?" Booker queries.

"Scare no one with a Cadillac," P. Washington declares.

"What's that *Khuhh-zar* look like?" Montgomery interjects. The woman's fingers are curled into the iron tulips, tearing at their rigid petals.

"They got one in there?" asks Booker.

"Is it bigger than the rhino?" calls Washington, skipping behind the lady.

"Where is he?" she cries, wheeling from the gate. The woman runs a few steps forward on her heels, which hook in the soft soil at the edge of the pavement.

"Who?"

"Is he in there?"

"The *Khuhh-zar*?"

"What's that thing look like?"

She turns to the right and sees Montgomery. Her hand grasps his coat collar and jerks him so close he can smell the heavy must of her perfume. His nose tickles. "Did you see him?" the woman in thick furs cries.

"Couldn't see one," whispers P. Washington. "He's been with us all day."

"I'm going to call the police," screams the lady.

Montgomery's left leg begins to tremble. P. Washington and T. Booker back off, ready to run but afraid to desert the playmate pinned by the lapel between the fingernails of the woman in black sealskins.

"Why do you want him?" asks Washington.

"He ran away?" adds Booker.

"You keep him locked up?" asks Montgomery.

The lady fixes an eye scalded with tears run dry on Richmond. Red circles are burnt into her pale flesh under a paste of eye shadow. She lets go of the child's coat.

"How'd he get away," asks Washington.

"He went. He just *went*." The lady speaks too loud. The boys can feel the animals in the cracked frieze wince.

"You didn't have him on a chain?" inquires Booker.

"I thought. I thought. He told me. Look!" She thrusts out her icy hand with the exclamation. The boys see a diamond acorn caught in the claws of a gold band.

"That's real," gasps Montgomery.

"No," she cries. "No, it wasn't real."

"How long is he gone?" Washington asks.

"Four years. Four years!" The buffalo shifts his hump on top of the Corinthian columns. The lioness snaps her tail.

"Why do you think he's here?" wonders Booker.

"They *told* me."

"Who?" cry the boys all together.

The woman turns her head from side to side. Wind blows through her open coat and she shivers.

"He got a tail?" asks Washington.

She shakes her head. "Claws?" "Four legs?" "Two?" She nods to the last as the voices mingle. "Like to climb trees, eat a lot of peanuts?" "Got hair all *over* him?" "Got a long beard?"

Again, she nods. "You looking for a *man?*" asks Booker.

The woman assents. "This *Khuhh-zar* is a …" They all burst into giggles, until they see the tears streaking colors down her cheeks. "You really …" "Want to get in?" "I know a hole …" "Under the fence …" The boys clamor to be first.

"C'mon," says Booker, taking the lady's hand. She yields to the tug and steps out on the grass, rounds the corner of the zoo's enclosure, a line of iron fence pikes.

"You got to get down and crawl," Richmond warns. "You will ruin your dress."

"All you got to do is put down a newspaper. Don't need to take a ten-mile hike round the whole park to get to *here*," says Washington. "Get that paper over there, Booker. She won't even dirty her nylons."

They arrive at a spot in the fence where a pile of leaves is heaped against the steel webbing of a cyclone barrier.

"This here is secret, ma'am. Don't tell anyone."

"Who's she going to tell?" Montgomery asks Washington. "Think she has a runny mouth, like you?"

"Like to have something running down your nose?" Washington warns, kicking among the leaves before the fence to reveal a space of two feet or so where an animal or boy has burrowed under the wire. Squatting, Washington slides through, followed by Booker. Richmond spreads papers on the dirt and shows the lady how to get down sinking to her belly and wriggle forward.

All four tiptoe over the grass, into the center of the mall, a long plain with a strip of sidewalk down the center. It is deserted, not a single baby carriage, couple, teenager, in sight. Far away, a single car starts up, disturbing the stillness.

"You married to this *Khuhh-zar*?" asks Washington. She nods.

Richmond blushes.

"He eats peanuts?" Washington inquires.

"I like 'em," Booker shouts.

"Let's look in the elephant's house!" cry the boys.

They swing left on the soft green and approach a squat building, glass domed with a crumbling pachyderm head over the door, seeping cement specks from the length of its curling trunk. "What's he doing in there?" asks Montgomery. "Think he's a baby like Booker? You are wasting this woman's time."

"You want to bet on that?" Washington asks.

"My momma told me not to make any bets with you."

"Momma's boy, Momma's boy, little Richmond's a Momma's boy!" sing Booker and Washington. The lady pats Montgomery's curls.

"Smell that elephant," Booker whistles.

"You ever see an elephant with one tusk and no trunk?" asks Richmond.

"He got hit by a truck," Booker huffs.

Inside the house of pachyderms, a huge rhinoceros and a hippo are tethered in one of the cages where the elephants are usually confined. A few wisps of straw, the husks of a dozen peanut shells, lie on the cracked concrete floor.

"Smell a *Khuhh-zar*?" giggles Washington.

"I told you we were fooling around. You are wasting …"

"You wait, Montgomery. Mr. Fletch! Hey Fletch! Fletch!" shouts Washington through an open door into the keeper's office.

"Leave them animals alone," rasps a voice from inside. "I'm goin' to throw you in and let them stomp."

"Fletcher. Mr. Fletcher! You seen a *Khuhh-zar*?"

"Watch your mouth!" the keeper responds. "You going to be hippo grits!"

"Have you seen him?" the woman cries, her high voice in the hot, musky den of elephants, ringing back from the stone walls.

A face crisscrossed with lines, appears in the keeper's doorway. Beer can in hand, his white cotton sleeveless underwear is stuffed into two pants legs, below a rumpled gray bag of stomach. "What you doin' with that white lady?"

"You know a man with a long beard?" blurts Washington.

"A big peanut eater," adds Booker.

"What color that beard be?"

"Black," calls the lady.

"I sure do know that man. About my height with shiny eyes and a black cap, sometimes be wearing little boxes on his head and arm, trailing a stringy black, white scarf?"

"Yes, yes," she assents.

"You know that man?" the Keeper asks.

"Yes! Yes!"

"Stay a-way. I don't want no trek with that man or his relatives. He sneaked right in between the bars, slippin' over to the elephants, hippo, rhino, you name the game, talking stuff, and made them beasts go crazy. Blowing, trumpeting till the whole house is shakin'. When they ship off the Indian elephants because they ain't African, he took up with the hippo. I find him he-ah with the rhino, stealin' peanuts and messin' round in their shit. Where is that man? I'm going to get my hands on him …"

"Where is he?" she pleads.

"I'd like to know. About a year, just before the beasts from India were to be de-poited someone tipped them off. They broke their chains, kicked down the back do-ah, headin' across Moi-ton Street, thundrin' toi-ed the Blue Hills. Had to round them up with garbage trucks. Sittin' twenty years shufflin' and depressed, then out of nowhere breaking out? Freedom now. It wasn't me. I told the park commissioner. You get the boy with the beard. Boy with a black beard, boxes on his head, arm, till the commissioner point' toi-wad Mattapan, and the nut house, I *know* to shut *my* mouth. You *know* that boy?"

"Yes, yes."

"She married to him," adds Booker.

A big grin breaks across the keeper, Mr. Fletcher's wrinkled face. "Mmm … mmm."

"You seen him lately, Mr. Fletcher?" asks Richmond.

"My mouth got me in trouble al-ready."

"Please," the woman says, "Please."

"You boys going to be my witnesses."

"Yes," they cry.

"You from welfare, social security, or po-lice, lady? Why should I peach on that boy?"

"Look at that ring," says Washington, "Ever see welfare come down your street with a ring like that?"

Booker T. lifts her arm, stretches it above his head to display the glittering wedge.

"You boys brought the genuine thing," Mr. Fletcher whistles. "You got your breath tight round your finger. What you walking round Roxbury in those furs anyway?" He shakes his head. "You kids are going to get yourself in trouble. Look at that ring … mmm. You boys gettin' paid by the hour?"

"Are you going to help us or not?" asks Washington.

"You this lady's a-ttoi-ney" Come back here, boy. I need an a-ssistant. Get in there with the rhino. I need a sweeper. You handle that rhino's blues?"

"Please," begs the woman wrapped in black furs.

"I'm going to help. To the limit of what I know, lady. If you want the boy with the black beard—it's been four weeks since I saw him."

"Where is he?"

"Only a few places the boy can be. Under the refectory in the cellar hole. Up in the ruins on Teacher's Hill. The cat house, pagoda, or … no." The zookeeper thinks for a moment. "I can smell when he come in here, right through the rhino and the elephant mess. He got an o-dor, damp, soggy, down below the root smell." He claps his hands.

"Down under the poiddin'stone is a cave, no natural hole, but deep, deep down. You check out the cat house, refectory, Teacher Hill, but finally you find yourself up in a wilderness, and look down a sewer."

"Up there in the woods?" asks Montgomery.

"Past the g ... g ... golf course?" squeaks Booker.

"That's right. Your momma let you go there?" Mr. Fletcher turns his eye from one to the other. The boys look down. He addresses the woman. "You going to take these boys—what their mommas say to you?"

"I'm no sissy," whispers Washington.

"What will your momma say, if this lad brings you back here with your eyes picked out?"

"You're the sissy."

"I am going to put you in there with the rhino," says Fletcher, stepping forward.

"Come on," says Washington. "I know where those woods are."

"You sure you don't want to leave that ring with me for safe keeping?"

They back out of the elephant house to his laughter. Outside they stand on the soft green grass.

"Why don't we look in the cat house first?"

"Locked up," says Booker.

"He told us anyway, we got to go to the woods."

"There's that gang up there."

"Are you going to leave this lady alone?"

"Where are the woods?" she asks. Washington points west where the treetops on the hills rise above the gates. She turns and runs down the asphalt path in that direction, leaving her other shoe stuck in the lawn.

"Ma'am, wait."

"Wait, wait," cries Montgomery, snatching up her heel.

They chase her black fur through the Roman statuary of the towering front gate, across a service road by the football stadium, across its parking lots, into the woods. Her outline is lost among the trees as they scramble up the rocky face of the Wilderness, following the crashing in the underbrush. Tumbling down a dip between two ridges, they see the tip of her seal whip around a boulder above their heads. The throb of a car muffler starts behind them.

Crouching, they watch an old black Cadillac roll out of its hiding place under a canopy of brush, the chrome bumpers newly polished and hear a voice just beside it in the bushes. "Did yuh see that fuhhr?"

The harsh Boston brogue is answered by a Southern accent. "Ah did! It's not off a bargain rack."

"You gonna?"

"Reilly." The limousine rolls out of earshot.

"Is that the gang?" whispers Montgomery. Washington hushes him. Squatting in a depression filled with oak leaves they watch the Cadillac turn onto the dirt road. A red-headed man in a torn plaid woolen jacket is jogging beside it.

• • •

"Sniff the ground." The Reverend Mustapha in striped pants, bursting buttons, vest, squeezed behind the steering wheel, whispers. Mustapha swings the wheel into the flesh of his stomach, backing the limousine between two beeches.

"I he-ah her. Cut de engine," Reilly answers. The latter has been relieving himself and his pants drop to his knees as he leans into the wind. As the throb dies, they can distinguish the scuffing of feet in the dry carpet of beech, pin oak, maple.

A barefoot woman in a heavy seal coat, her blanched face glowing with violent red lipstick, stares at them from forty feet away. "Well hello, honey," calls the Reverend. "Come on over here. Daddy can help you." She continues to stare, "Ah can't hear you, honey dew." Struggling past the wheel, he clicks the car door open. "Come a little closer."

"Run," cries a chorus from the bushes.

"Whose 'at?" Reilly jerks his head about as the woman bolts into the underbrush.

"Git Reilly," the Reverend calls as he slams the car door and starts down the dirt road. "Beat the bushes. I'm going to cut her off."

The fur wiggles down between the rocks, but Reilly catches up with the rabbi's wife and reaches for her calf when a sharp stone strikes him on the cheek. A fistful of pebbles, sand, explodes in his face. Blinded, he roars, whirling around, hits his head on a puddingstone knob, as a stick slices across his nose. He seizes a thin wrist, a child's. About to snap it something bites him and then a rock knocks him down. When he picks himself up, he hears the noise of saplings far below him. He runs to the left, confused by the direction of the sound when the purr of the Cadillac's horn far off calls him to the playing field.

Too Irish

The young man about to be thrown into the pudding is sitting on a horse, long baton in reach of his fingers, pistol strapped to his side.

McShane has been dispatched to Franklin Park—the closest wilderness at hand. His supervisor, the captain of the local precinct, confided to his desk sergeant, "The boy is befuddled." McShane was *too* Irish. Well and good to greet your superiors in Gaelic, but a prospectus for Celtic worship on the bulletin board? The officer combined two fine qualities, tenderheartedness and rectitude, but was perverse in applying them. Sent out on the paddy wagon, he protested as his fellows beat the recreational boozers into pulp. On foot patrol, he reported partners in the collection of weekly, monthly and holiday gratuities. He volunteered an embarrassment of information to his sergeant, lieutenant, which the captain did not want to hear about even in the form of anecdote. "A good boy, bright," everyone allowed, but one who had missed his "vocation." Neither church nor department of welfare would be interested in "the red cow of Kerry," hero of an epic he was scribbling in his notebook, *The Táin Bo East Broadway.*

How had he gotten into the force? The records seemed to be in order but something in the applications troubled the captain whenever he fingered the file on McShane. The documents that spilled out were perfectly ordinary, but it was hard to focus on the handwriting. Sleep fogged the captain's eyes whenever he tried to and he found himself waking up to drop the folder back into his metal cabinets. McShane had to be provided for like any of the others, the alcoholics, the sadists, the light fingered, the hasty tempered, the depressed: those whose disabilities did not absolutely disqualify them for police duty.

Not a single officer would share a car with McShane. Some liked him, but confessed to the desk sergeant, "Can't afford it." His uncanny hearing made him a danger in the station house. It was genius on the captain's part, met with tears of gratitude and congratulations the staff, when he docked McShane's pay for the rental of a superannuated horse from the local stable and let the officer ride up and down the park's paths on his tour of duty. The creature, hardened during his professional life between the shafts of a junkman, could endure showers of stone, nails, air gun pellets. As it poked in the shrubbery McShane astride, sexual molesters, pickpockets, muggers, flower children come to disrobe under the skies, scattered. The steed created the deepest discouragement to malefactors in lifting a hoof and threatening to discharge his weapon.

• • •

Looking down from the clouds over Boston, the horizon to the south showing the shape of the Great Blue Hill, the sun sinks into its fleecy bed like the flanks of a red cow in the policeman's eye, as he notes as well a furry dot streaking across the green of the golf course, followed by a black Cadillac. Another figure, a flash of white sticks below a red patch of jacket, runs in a half circle about the hairy point. Other shadows too flicker on the emerald playing field.

• • •

Now comes the clash of arms, jangling harness, squeak of rubber spheres, slam of horseflesh on the green grass. A lady runs in circles, furs abandoned on the lawn, barefoot, screaming before a naked nimbus. In the final yards of his headlong rush, the blue policeman draws out a short hickory nightstick and cracks the bog troll, whom he identifies, and shouts, "O'Reilly!" One rap across the skull and the criminal falls tangled in his own soiled underwear.

But before the blue man can dismount, embrace the barefoot lady—with a rumble and glitter of chrome a black Cadillac slams into rider and horse.

White feet stained with green, scratched, bloody, over the stones of Nazingdale the lady runs to make her escape. Three boys rise from a hollow in the ground to conduct her but over the silent field comes a crackling voice. "Woman, what are you doin'—catching a cold? Where is your seal? "

There is a tinkle of glass. "Bring that young lady with you."

The dark shadow, which appeared on the edge of the accident, begins to tiptoe away.

"Fletcher, stop. You got a debt of ten thousand owed me, the day your animals all went lame at Suffolk Downs. I don't want to but you got a short straw and my word is all that stands between you and a final settlement." The barrel of a sawed-off shotgun protrudes through the broken windshield. Three shorter shadows sink back into the depths of a sand trap. The lady stands frozen in a pool of blood bubbling from the horse's mouth.

"Pluck up that sugar plum."

Fletcher reaches, the woman jumps away, whirls and begins to flee. "Don't shoot," he calls. "Don't shoot. I'll catch her"

"Get in," shouts Mustapha. The supine body of Reilly flung in the rear seat, the preacher races after the woman, Fletcher hanging on the running board.

They speed over the silken nub of the putting circle, lurch out onto the fairways, would have overtaken the fugitive in seconds but a rear tire striking the edge of a sand pit, the car spins around, skidding, filling the front seat with fine stinging dust. The Cadillac heels in the air, and when they come down, Fletcher is calling, "Wait up, wait up, Momma!" It is hard to see more than the woman running in front. Leaning out, the zoo keeper has her by the waist, but the brakes fail. Runner and automobile breast the waters of Scarboro Pond, briefly in turmoil, then slowly calm.

Dusk falls on Franklin Park. A few faint stars shine above the grass of the fairway. Far from the road, horse and rider lie matted in the brush. Three children are running toward a police phone, dodging their own reflections.

"You going to let the lady drown," speaks a watery bulk rising out of the pond.

"Can't find her," Fletcher spits out with a mouthful of the oozy pond.

"Look at me," Mustapha begs the dummy in his arms, wiping sedge from Reilly's eyes. A tangle of skirts floats to the surface.

Slowly the woman opens her eyes. She looks up at the wizened face that leans over her as she lies on her back in the grass. "I am the keeper," whispers Fletcher.

"Whose keeper?"

"Your keeper, honey." She takes his hand and presses it.

"You all right, honey? C'mon, get up off that cold ground. You goin' to catch your death lying damp, half naked." Fletcher draws her up, his hand locked tight in hers. She sees the preacher and shivers.

"Are you going to keep me?"

"I said I would, Momma."

"I'm your momma," she says, kissing Fletcher's cheek.

"Baby," Fletcher says, "you make me feel silly."

"How can I be your momma and your baby?"

"You be whatever you want to."

"I want to be a baby."

"Oh Lord," cries Mustapha. "We don't have time for baby talk."

Sirens are wailing in the skies of Boston.

• • •

The phone rang in the Jamaica Plain Precinct. "Lady just kidnapped!" squealed a child into the phone.

Another high pitched voice shouted into the receiver, "Cadillac sunk. They got dunked!"

A third slightly lower, cut in, "Hit that horse right on!"

"Who is it?" the captain who happened to be passing, asked.

"Some little hoodoos from Roxbury," answered the desk sergeant, putting his palm over the mouthpiece. "I'll give 'em a scare." The officer took his hand off the mouthpiece. "*A horse's ass!*" he bawled into the receiver. "*I know you kids.*"

"Right, he hit it in the *be-hind*," one of the children squealed.

"You seen it *too*?" added another.

"That policeman is dead on the ground," chimed the third.

"*Policeman*?" One shocked voice after another echoed in the sudden silence of the precinct.

"Lying in the grass."

"Dead as the horse."

Individual voices were lost in the sudden tumult through the station house.

• • •

Father S. J. O'Halloran, claiming he was the family's oldest friend, met the mob of the reporters at the door of the hospital room, waved them back before they could see what they hoped to pop pictures of, a mummy suspended by a host of fine wires. O'Halloran motioned them to the far end of the corridor, shutting the door firmly behind, twirling the key. At last S. J. had a saint firmly under lock and key. In the past twenty-four hours everyone in the city had been trying to get into the hospital and to the bedside: bask in the radiance despite the doctors' strict orders, no admittance, even family. S. J. had slipped in claiming he was a missionary doctor, and threatening the hospital's accreditation. The mayor had come in on the last tack alone.

His Honor shed copious tears at the emergency entry though he had banished the boy from the center of Boston himself for indiscriminate ticketing. Of the trio who had been in the room beside the doctors and police, His Eminence was the only one sent for and he hadn't known the lad was in town. The cardinal had long ago ordered him off the force in the wake of several socialist tracts, announcing the New Fenians, traced to McShane's locker. Now the prelate hurried to the quarantined room at City Hospital, turning a grim face from the photographers who were thrust abruptly out of his path. The whole city was a-shake.

An Irish cop killed, or almost, in *Roxbury*? Run down? "Underhanded, insidious, the most consummate heartlessness this city has known since the day of the Boston Massacre," declaimed a rival of the mayor from the top of a truck strung with loudspeakers to the crowd swelling at the hospital steps. "Then it was the *red* coats, now it's the bla-bbblaa …" His Eminence threw the candidate a dirty look that made his shrill voice falter. But every bar in South Boston, Celtic Dorchester, Rosindale, Jamaica Plain, was lit up like a Christmas tree, choleric. A holy war was about to begin. Bicycle chains, BB guns, souvenirs of the Korean Conflict, howitzers, were brought out. It was like the old days thought S. J., when from Saint Leo's church in the middle of Jewish streets he sent the kids out to set the score straight on the Savior's sheet, rub a little vinegar into the crown of that arrogant nation. Now, bedad, the legions of Ham were rising up. It was a chance to strike primeval Babylon, hit the old snake on the head. There were too few Jews for a fair fight citywide but now, white versus black. The Gaelic blood was up. "Up. Up, the Savior's cup!" he shouted into the amazed face of the cardinal as the latter retreated from the room. S. J. tugged at his hand.

"I thought dey retired you to Arizonah, O'Halloran?"

"This is the last chance for an Irish Boston," the retired priest whispered in the mayor's ear as that dignitary shook him off coming out of Seamus' room.

• • •

Paddy wagons, squad cars, ambulances, a tank from the Boston armory: half a regiment of state troopers, converged on the fallen horse and rider. Spotlights shivered the dark. The banshee wailed over Blue Hill Avenue.

"D … D … Don't listen."

His five senses knocked to the winds, Seamus' skull received the trickle of a voice, dripping drop by drop into the broad crack in his cranium.

Before the policeman, a doctor was kneeling with his stethoscope. "Is the boy alive or dead?" barked a cap decked with gold braid.

The doctor motioned with his hand to be quiet. "Well," cried the captain after a minute or two.

"Feel the pulse for yourself," said the doctor, intent on his stethoscope.

The blue official gingerly put his fingers on the limp wrist of Seamus. He tried to pick it up. The arm, heavier than lead, would not rise.

"What's this?" he inquired.

"Feel."

The policeman put his finger to the vein under the thumb. "There's no pulse."

"D … D … Did you ever hear of Sh … Sh … Sheba?"

Why should he hear of Sheba? Akiba, his *kop* is full of Mooney. Looney Tuney. You're wasting your time. Leave the boy alone. What does he want with black queens? Bad enough she's tickling you and me. Keep the *Shechinah* to yourself. Pray the officer goes back unwashed to the living.

"He's dead," wailed the captain.

"No, no," insisted the doctor from the ground. "I hear something in his chest."

"No pulse," said the captain.

"I know. Listen …" The physician pulled the stethoscope out of his ear and stuck it in the captain's.

"H … H … He clings to you. H … H … He desires i … i … instructions."

Akiba. Akiba. Always after disciples. You put your tooth in his ear. Forty thousand from your *chedar* up and down the length of the land like Hillel, anyone who could stand on one leg would be hopping after you. Why do you start with this cop? If we begin to instruct, we are responsible. Revive the soul of the horse. It had a Jewish upbringing. Understands a little Yiddish; doesn't know pork.

"What's this?" exclaimed the officer.

"Do you hear a thump, thump, thump?" inquired the medical professional.

"No. Wait, yes—that's a heartbeat!"

"Thump, thump?" asked the doctor.

"Yes," said the captain, puzzled.

"A heartbeat?"

"Yes, well …" The police official's face grew perturbed as he listened.

"What's it sound like?"

"I don't know."

"An echo," snapped the doctor, seizing the stethoscope. He plugged it back into his ear. "A beep. Sonar. Music, the heart muscle is throbbing like a larynx."

"Back, back, back," growled the captain, his face flushed purple, spreading his gold-laced cuffs to the side, pushing the crowd of policemen who were pressing in on the stricken body suddenly. "Back."

"He's smiling," they whispered. "Smiling." the lips of the comatose man had imperceptibly drawn up at the corners.

Several policemen stiffened in the ranks.

"Aaaaaagh," a scream sent sick chills screeching down the constabulary's spines.

"It's the banshee," a voice in the deep blue press announced.

"Pick him up," ordered the captain. "You, you, you," his finger signaled a dozen of the tallest in the files around the body.

"Don't," shouted the doctor. "Don't even try."

• • •

The mayor slammed the door in Father O'Halloran's face, keeping his hand locked on the doorknob so the lock behind His Honor stayed in place. He could feel the priest trying frantically to turn and un-jam it. The noise of O'Halloran's banging could hardly be heard in the uproar of reporters.

"The doctors tell me the boy's condition is stable," said the mayor. "Immovable, neither up or down for the last forty-nine hours."

"Is it critical?" called a tenor from the *Boston Globe*.

"I tell you the truth, off the record, all I can get out of the doctor is some gibberish about traumas and dislocation of encephalograms, damn …"

"Is he alive?" piped a falsetto from the *Italian-American Gazette*.

"Who paid you?" O'Blank shouted at the tiny man in frayed pants and jacket. The mayor's red cheeks drained of color as he looked icily at the part-time reporter. "Who put a ten-dollar bill in your pocket?"

The dwarf took a step back. "There's water under the basement of your printing press," the mayor added. "You better keep an eye on the plumbing. Lot of flooding in East Boston ... Now," his voice a wide, balmy breeze, the mayor intoned, "a great load of responsibility ..." The volume rose as the reporters quieted down in the hospital corridor and the hammering behind him grew more insistent. "Rests on all of us in public service, and especially the press, in the next few weeks to keep the peace. Unscrupulous agitators, madmen of all creeds and denominations are seeking to take advantage of this unspeakable tragedy. The dastards who did this will feel the heavy hand ..." The banging rose above his voice, which had dropped to give rhetorical stress to the sentence.

"Someone's trying to get out of that room."

"Have I done you boys a lot of favors?" asked the mayor, his voice a zephyr off the old chocolate factory in Lower Mills. He eyed several key men in the crowd. "Today I'm asking you, quietly, to depart this corridor. You are disturbing the rest of this brave officer. Ordinarily, you know I'm in favor of full publicity. *Now*, for the sake of the city, we ..." he waved his fingers at the detectives in his entourage to start pushing the reporters toward the hospital elevators, "*has* to exercise responsibility. Respon—." Both hands swung open in his victory salute, blessing the reporters as they were herded.

The door swung open in the second's lapse. The mayor staggered to the side. "Burn," was howled at the press. "Burn Boston. Burn."

Flailing a lump of sod, O'Halloran charged into the elevator, was down the shaft and out the door before the detectives caught in the mob rushing back toward the door of the stricken officer's room could set their wits straight. The mayor was ahead of everyone, bolting the door. He cried out to the journalists trying to get in and see for themselves, "Over my dead body."

• • •

His arm entwined in loops and circles of gold, curling snakes of braid, a tall figure stepped forward among the blue men gathered on the grass. He addressed the man in white cloth bending over the prostrate body. "Mae ef yn ddn na welais!"

The captain and other officers heard with astonishment, the doctor reply, "Crdwn ninnau hynny," to Finn, commissioner of the Boston Police Force. Descended in a line of forty-three elder sons from Finnebennach Ai, pig keeper of the king of the *sidh* in Connacht, the commissioner's career had been marked by missing pages out of the police blotter, inscrutably brilliant civil service examinations, a plague clearing the way for his advancement. He had only to breath the body odor of the attending physician to know him as forty-third in a line of the youngest sons of the "dark brown dire haughty" pig keeper to the king of the Munster *sidh*. What brought the two face-to-face? Seamus, whom

Finn had protected, was the middle child in as many generations of the daughters of Queen Medb.

Loops of gold writhed on the commissioner's wrists. The ends lashed above his elbows. "It seems to me," he continued, waving his men out of earshot, "that the child is unnatural in his attachment to this park."

"You have struck it exactly."

"He will not come away from it."

"Not by a pig's bristle."

"This is past understanding."

"A pungent truth."

"A whiff of it would render the city senseless."

The nose of the doctor assented.

"I am putrid with the thought of it."

The doctor opened his palms and shook them in front of his nostrils.

"There is still one course open to us."

The fingers froze.

"Let us remove him from the damp face of the heavens and the chill of the wet grass."

The palm waved as if to inquire the way.

"Since we are not on the soil of the Celts but among Sumerians, Assyrians, Hebrews, we must seek help in the holy number seven to sever this Gael from the sod."

Minutes later, seven shovels played in the frozen earth sprinkling gravel, showering stone, the doctor, the commissioner. A sharp keening burst from the rocks at the edge of the golf course. Hawks and owls fluttered in the sky above them. Drums sounded in the streets off the park, deep hollow logs of maple and oak as if animal skins had been stretched across. The commissioner and his sergeants lifted the seven-foot sod out of the ground in one sliver and slid it onto the oversized stretcher from Boston City Hospital.

"Sheba!" wailed in the wind.

• • •

A phone rang in the sleeping policeman's room at the hospital. The mayor had been fiddling with the earth under the body. It was hard as conglomerate. How did they ever hack it out, he wondered as he lifted the receiver. "You backed the wrong horse," he heard Father S. J. O'Halloran cackle. Bells went off in the mayor's brain. He held the earphone, hearing the Father click off. Dazed for a moment, he hung up and dialed the commissioner. The snakes hissed on the chief's right arm as he held the receiver to his ear. He had accounted for six responsibilities of his, His Honor the mayor, His Eminence the cardinal, his cohort the doctor, he himself, and his officer in the hospital bed, his antagonist, O'Halloran, only ...

"What horse?" asked the mayor.

"Where is it?" cried the commissioner in alarm.

"What?"

"His horse!"

"You mean *his* horse?" The mayor was puzzled.

"*His!*'

"The dump."

"Hurry."

"Why?"

"O'Halloran's after it."

"Why?" It made no sense to His Honor.

"He's after it."

"Why?"

Flinging down the phone, the commissioner rushed out his office door. The seven sergeants detailed to him since their dig followed, running toward his Cadillac paddy wagon. They flew with sirens screeching toward the dump at Franklin Park. A sick heart told him what he would find—tracks of a truck and a mocking sign. He should have shut O'Halloran up until he had solved the riddle. Now it was all too clear. "Swear out a warrant!" the commissioner had called back to the dangling receiver.

"For what?"

"A horse," he bellowed. "A dead horse." He smelled the end of the city.

The Green Horse

Boston was full of gas.

It was not Saint Patrick's fault.

Was it the cardinal's fault?

Not the mayor's—. Who could predict a dead nag would ride into the heavens?

After they hustled the policeman in, O'Halloran had thought of rushing to the hospital. He would snatch Seamus and the sod he was stuck to, set up a basement chapel. But the priest didn't have enough support yet in the Irish streets. And moldy cellar prayers were the cardinal's specialty. S. J. wanted to be out in the open, on the march.

The horse of the cop was dead. Therefore its resurrection could not be questioned. And the harder the mayor tried to hide its rider, Seamus, the more mysterious the whole thing. Let them enshrine the battered policeman in a hospital, walled into a cell. One couldn't do anything with a body nobody would believe was dead. The horse, however, was stiff as an old two-by-four. Gone—anyone within forty feet could smell that.

But if the police got their noses on it prematurely, the jig was up.

The first order of business after rescuing the cadaver was to tone down its odor and preserve its flesh against the day.

S. J. organized a hit and run on Donovan's funeral home, stole twenty gallons of embalming fluid, taking Donovan along to fix the corpse. The funeral director refused to participate until they strapped his son into a chair, started pouring sand and water. "It's a long way to Tipperary," hummed O'Halloran. His aides giggled about the bottom of the bay while junior's sneakers trembled in a cement tub. "We know all about you, the North End bookies, and that crook, Lennie the *Shtoup*. You've embalmed the worst beasts in Boston. Half the getaway cars in the metropolis fit the digits on your limousines' plates. Get busy with the animal. I want it to stand up straight, striking an attitude of piety with an impression of rigor."

Handkerchief up his nose soaked in cologne, Donovan went to work with a water pump. It was too risky to bring the horse to the funeral home. The police commissioner, Finn, had gotten wind of Donovan's disappearance within hours and posted a guard around the white frame of the seven-gabled house of interment. Detectives after O'Halloran went from bar to bar, Houlihan's, Beach Tavern, Tom English's, The Quencher, Cassidy's, Sonny & White's, The Coachman, buying drinks, setting up the counter with the best. Riff raff slopped up the liquor but neither threats nor promises could shake out a word of the missing horse.

As Finn drove up to Donovan's to check the cordon of detectives, someone threw a bottle at his squad car. The cardinal reported a slump in the collection boxes. Authority was crumbling. The word was going round, O'Halloran's got his horse. Even the men on the force were growing restive. The city council had shifted to O'Halloran's side. His Honor was tap dancing on the desk when the commissioner arrived.

"What's up?"

"Keeping on my toes."

"Yer going to be on your bottom, if you don't watch out."

"I'm going to stay up in the air," His Honor retorted, doing a kick that levitated both heels high over the green leather blotter. "No help for it. The wind is shifting."

"You've got to come down to earth," barked Finn. "You've got to take a stand."

"Oh no," cried the mayor, gaily. "You don't catch me there," as the commissioner made a grab for his ankles. "I gave you two weeks to nab that priest. Come up with the horse. There's a statue of limitations."

"Give me another week. I'll smell him out."

"Too late," snapped His Honor, executing a set of hand springs—the tips of his pumps ricocheting off the ceiling. "He and his horse can come into the open. I can't hold out against public opinion. I'll have to be the first to shake his hand."

"He'll burn your town down."

The mayor went in concentric circles upside down around the brilliant chandelier. The crystals tinkled musically. Finn stalked out, slamming the door behind him. On his head, His Honor steadied himself in place, tapping the wall by the ringing telephone. Finally, he picked up the receiver and began to explain his position to the puzzled governor.

Still, thought the commissioner, there's the cardinal.

"I can't do anything," His Eminence confessed in a dusty box at the back of the cathedral where both had agreed to meet.

Everyone had turned into a spy for O'Halloran. Finn was disguised with a long white wig in a dirty dress and lady's handbag. "Can't you excommunicate him?"

"It's all I can do to keep the horse from being canonized. Not a single coin has come into the collection boxes since he waylaid that animal."

"He's smarter than I gave him credit for."

"He'll catch himself up," comforted the cardinal.

• • •

"Hocus pocus," cried O'Halloran. His Eminence must have some curse congealing against him in the cathedral's communion cup. They had pumped embalming fluid until they could have immortalized a herd of wild stallions. The smell persisted and thrilled his own nose, pickled against the world's stench through seventy years of Irish whiskey and malt. Donovan was on the floor, dead away. Coughing, O'Halloran had to drag the undertaker up the stairs from the cellar where he had been operating on the horse. A hanger on, draped over the banister, intoned hoarsely, "Sugah cure." "Yes," the priest replied. Sacks of sugar slid down the coal chute from the Domino factory seemed to do the trick. "It's sweeter," O'Halloran sang as drops of caramel blistered on the upstairs linoleum. The hairs of his nose were clotted with black bits of sugar. He shook the shoulder of Donovan who had been hung out a second floor window for air.

"I can taste it out here," the latter wheezed.

"Sort of a perfume," S.J. replied. "A fragrant incense of roses."

"More like a rotten fish with a sweet tooth." The undertaker was yanked back in and marched downstairs. The horse stood in the cellar, its hide steaming. "Too sweet."

O'Halloran had to agree. "Where can we put it so no one can smell."

"Bury it," Donovan growled.

"Sink it," someone volunteered.

"That's it," said O'Halloran. "Donovan, is it waterproof?"

"Absolutely," answered the undertaker, pinching the horsehair. "We can swab it with silicone just to make sure."

The word went out. Southie would walk the waves. Meanwhile the sheriff of Suffolk County called to assure S. J. that all the warrants for him and the horse, had been recalled. S. J. was free to proceed.

A green stain spread out of the brackish brine of the Fort Point Channel. Schools of fish washed up, sweet to the point of putrid, the odor poisoned the salt breeze off Boston. The storm clouds and squalls over the city were tinted with emerald. Scavengers appeared in the harbor, oversized squid and sharks. Creatures of the depths surfaced on the mucky sands at Malibu, City Point, L Street, scrabbling with tentacles and fins over the shattered glass, bottle caps, beer cans, in their greed to swallow up the sticky corpses of mackerel, pollack, gasping in the tide. The commissioner wandered along Carson Beach, kicking violent kelly-colored jellyfish. He had asked his men to drop a depth charge but they couldn't acquire the explosives.

O'Halloran could crank the horse right under Finn's nose. Mayor, city council, the sewer commissioners, all were caught in the priest's net. They had consented, with enthusiasm, to his scheme, an *Extermination Day Parade*. "Exterminate who, what?" Finn bawled at the mayor, sniffing from the sugar left by S. J.'s skirts, that his opponent had just been in His Honor's chambers.

"Crime?" the mayor called from the chandelier.

"You can't exterminate crime!"

"A few criminals then," offered the officeholder.

• • •

O'Halloran was jumpy. "If a hair of that horse is out of place, you and your kid are going to the bottom of Fort Point." They were hoisting the steed up from the old ship channel by South Station where Colonel O'Cann, Ret., U.S.M.C. was standing beside him. A tug was submerged just under the railroad bridge to keep the police launch of the commissioner out. The streets buzzed angrily. Crowds of teenagers, from South Boston's, Eastie, Rosindale, Dorchester, and Upham's Corner, companies of young delinquents out of Everett, Malden, Chelsea, Charleston, were forming up along the avenue of the march. The sheriff at Suffolk Jail had given furloughs for the day to his inmates. Many who had not tasted the salt air for months were seen choked at the collar in uniforms of honorary marshals, green jackets just that morning unloaded from the Turnpike Authority. Colonel O'Cann had addressed the recruits in the dawn under the tin roof of a train shed. "You are a sorry bunch."

Laughter through unshaven ranks.

"Yuh know the real crooks!"

A chorus rattled the tin roof. "Hey. Hey. The cops today."

"Sergeant?" Skinny O'Toole who had been blown up in 1918 rigging a homemade bomb in the cooking line of the Cunard Liner taking him to France, rolled out a dolly with boxes of hardwood baseball bats, stuck through the crown with a six-inch spike. "Keep it under your coat. I'm giving you twelve inches of hickory and six of steel over the longest nightstick in South Boston." Grabbing a bat, O'Cann called, "Up the Irish! Sergeant!"

"Forward march." Platoons crossed the Fort Point Channel to take up stations in South Boston. Each man had a green cockamamie stamped on his forehead. Breaking off in groups of twos and threes, they sauntered up smirking to the blue coats the commissioner had strung at sunrise through the streets.

The police were stretched thin. Dozing off the liquor in the backseats of battered Fords and Chevrolets, parked in the side streets, hardly dampened by an all-nighter, drunk gangs of toughs had assembled. With the sun, more poured in from Waltham, Somerville, Watertown, smelling of puke and talcum. The paddy wagon wailed back and forth as they hurled curses at the police, dared them to take a swing. The downtown precincts' cells were clotted with champions urinating. The desk sergeants' feet were swiveled up on the blotter. "No more," they cried on the telephone. "No more room. Knock 'em down there! Stuff them. Don't bring another body."

A crew of gap-toothed marshals deployed itself on street corners of the parade and officers began to recognize faces. "O'Casey, didn't I put you away for the year? Milligan, are you out?" The bulletin up on the board last night had already unnerved them. "Take along a piece of metal in your pocket. Beware of hares. Don't look on a red-haired woman." It was a brave man who hadn't spilled a clip into his pants. The police shifted clanking to face the green newcomers.

Residents glared from the windows. Despite brothers, cousins, grandchildren on the force, the heroes of these streets were safecrackers, bank robbers—whatever wee trickster crept out from under the stiff net of lace curtain to enliven the turf. "The police are bank guards for the Yankees! Lickspittles to John Hancock, Prudential, State Street Trust! Fearful to go into Roxbury on foot patrol! Their own Seamus lies senseless at City Hospital. The shame of it—*castrati*—a chorus to a mayor who sold his manhood in the vault of the First National!" S. J. harangued from Carson Beach to Fort Point. Several lads had taken matters into their own hands—almost shoved a sour, black elder into the path of a speeding subway train. "Shake them up!"

Martial spirit however, infused the latter. A few hours later, some boys from Roxbury grabbed a Celtic reveler on the rocks at Columbia Point and sent him to teach the fishes. "Where is the commissioner? Milky bulletins—cool heads—keep your countenance. Speak again," shouted S. J. from his box in Perkins Place. Crowds were growing. A squad of strong-arm men surrounded him so they could whisk the priest away at the first sight of the commissioner. The blood was boiling up East Broadway and in the side streets, Story, Viking, Vicksburg, Bay streets. Wasn't it enough they were all mortgaged to the Pilgrims up in Pride's Crossing? Bradfords, Cabots, Lowells, Winthrops, the Yankees rubbing the salt in—their hearts bled for these new arrivals—once more, "Irish to the back of the line!"

"Shocking," the papers lectured the poor white inhabitants of Boston.

"Shocking?" That was an understatement. The Africans were stealing all the sympathy. They were shipping Blacks into the local social club, South Boston High. Hadn't the school committee signaled, appointing a basketball coach as superintendent of schools, that public education was a form of entertainment? The cardinal was ready with a scholarship to parochial school for anyone who wanted to seriously learn. There was even a Boston Latin School for Jews, Greeks, poor Protestants and recalcitrant Catholics. Who would send anyone for an education into South Boston? Shame and delusion! The straw on the camel's back burst into flame. "Extermination Day!" announced S. J. "The horse will rise, beast of the martyr from the waves. Southie shall be free. Here we go!"

"Here we go," roared the crowd. "Here we go Southie." The cops quivered at the edge of a blot of people spread out from the subway station at Broadway. A white-haired lady ran along their ranks shaking her umbrella. Beer cans in hand, thousands were shoving to get a better view; elbowing each other off the railroad tracks into the channel from bridges and stone walls as to a cranking of ropes and pulleys slung round the iron wheels of the old coal chutes, squealing, from a pea soup of sewage they drew ears, nostril, chest, and hooves, Seamus' mount, emerald, rose above the waves, the sun reflected off its glossy surface so brightly, the onlookers had to shield their eyes. "Three traits of a bull—a bold walk, a strong neck and a hard forehead; three traits of a fox—a light step, a look to the front, and a glance to each side of the road; three traits of a woman—a broad bosom, a slender waist, and a short back …"

The skirl of pipes called out as the horse was set down on the deck of Foundry Street, three times the size of the gray Clydesdales who drew the Budweiser Beer wagon. Tears bubbled in the eyes of the beholders—its smell like tear gas—while a green wind flapped the pipers' skirts.

Its hooves bounced once, twice, on the asphalt, rigid in rigor mortis, yet light on iron shoes. Donovan had stolen a leaf out of the mummy maker's manual. The horse could come down the avenues of South Boston neither reclining in a bier nor set on wheels, but floating, knocking its hooves on the cobbles, drawn by an honor guard of seven presumptive virgins from Seventh Street, cheerleaders of the soccer team from Gate of Heaven. To the pipes, drums, bugles, boom of the kettle, the crowd started after the horse and the floats of the home and school associations, neighborhood drill teams, a glut of piccolos, clarinets, tubas, all mixed up and moving backward over the Saint Patrick's/Evacuation Day Parade route. They began at the point of dismissal and rolled down West and East Broadway, then twisted into the smaller streets. A nun with a bullhorn was trying to order the units. Her coif slipped away revealing a swath of red hair. The police turned a deaf ear to her pleas. "Green marshals, green marshals!" she shrieked.

The march, swollen by Somerville, Quincy, Hingham, Dedham, Cambridge, Malden, turbulent elements of their junior and senior high school populations, Brighton, Jamaica Plain, the North End, streamed into a procession in which onlookers and participants were overwhelmed. Belligerent parents flowed into it from the side streets. They overwhelmed the stands and the city councilors, school committeemen, registrars of deed, district attorneys, congressmen, the secretary of state, lieutenant governor, state legislators, were swept along out of the shadow of the municipal courthouse with its squadron of tactical police force and the U.S. Ranger battalion crouched in the basement. It was a pell-mell of scrambling chaos along the march. "Stop it," a grey-haired lady was screaming, but her cry was one among thousands. The police cordon had disappeared in the first push. A helicopter swooped down with a snapping line and a single dignitary snatching at the end of it was swung up over the heads of the tumult, minus his striped trousers, shredded by those trying to cling to his coattail. His Honor giddy, jigging with bony shanks, up in the air, was in his element.

The horse loomed larger above the crowd. It had ballooned to several times its size since first striking hooves above the waves of Fort Point. Now it surged ahead.

In its wake—a swarm! They had been promised an orderly Extermination Day. S. J. had given his word. No racial epithets. Keep on the "criminal" theme. A quiet neighborhood demonstration! A former nun, enlisted in his cause, had scouted the parishes, waiting in the rectory bushes to carry off all the sore losers in the Holy Name Society and creating ad hoc Councils of Safety throughout the diocese. Placards jammed the streets. "CLEAN UP THE CRIMINALS." "SAFE STREETS." "DRIVE OUT THE DIRT FROM DORCHESTER." "SPOTLESS SOUTHIE." "SHAMROCK SOLID." "MURDER THE MURDERERS." But most of all, sprinkled with clover petals: "EXTERMINATE!" For days they had been weaving massive floats out of acres of crepe paper, the art of the home & school associations, thousands of crinkly artificial blossoms spelling, repeating, four-story festoons, sod houses, the Georgian lines of South Boston High, recreated with a slogan burning above the columned entry, "Exterminate."

The angry parents had expected to register their insistence on the mayor and council standing at attention on the courthouse steps. All order was swallowed up in the confusion as the trailers bearing the floats churned through a battle of fists between protesters and revelers moving on after the horse. The mayor swinging like a trapeze artist, blowing kiss after kiss to the civil servants he recognized below, looping home to city hall, was the final blow. The parents struck out right and left at everyone with a grin on his face, or a can in hand.

There were crooks everywhere. Green men were snatching handbags right and left. Hardly a pocket was left unpicked. South Boston had become a hornet's nest. Bats with nails waved through the air. The streets were slippery with blood and there were Easter bunnies underfoot making the ladies crazy. "Police!" was the cry on all sides. "Police!"

"I can't shoot lady, it's too tight."

"Me shells are in me pocket."

"Milligan, Milligan."

"Oh God, me toe, me toe." A sea of elbows and fists were pushing and shoving in every direction, but the thrust was forward.

"That horse is getting too big," S. J. called. Far ahead he could see the glistening flanks, smooth and swollen as a blimp, stuck. It was wedged just in front of the firehouse, between two three-deckers at the turn of the parade from East Sixth into K Street. "Don't push. Don't push."

Hundreds of thousands were being pushed, by trucks, bayonets, drill teams, behind them. "Push 'em back, push 'em back, *waaaaay* back." The football cheer came from the crowd. The buoyant horse rebounded the shove like a shock absorbing trampoline. A wave bowled thousands over. "Here we go *Southie*," howled the mob, scrambling up, shoving. "Here we *go*!" The three deckers trembled. The pipes shrilled. The horse shook.

"Fire! Fire!" An alarm went off and the engines pushed from the firehouse into the fray. An old lady with a soiled dress, waving a skinny umbrella wiggled her way madly through the assemblage locked in the struggle, squeezed under the belly of the beast and with her furled rain gear, thrust up into the animal.

Bang!

A slender column on top of which a mushroom of green gas thickened, crowned Boston. The commissioner ascended leaving wig and dress behind on the firehouse roof as proof of his apotheosis. Seven of his sergeants were sucked up too. The boom resounded from Bunker Hill and rang the harbor bells out beyond Boston Light. The wonder stilled every tongue. Irradiated by the green horse as the fallout rained down, only slowly did they realize what happened. On every face staring up, a stain of green so deep appeared that for all apparent purposes they were black as Africans.

It took weeks of hiding in the shade of apartments before splotches of pale skin broke through. The smell of gas clung to their skins, scrub as they might and for months to come cousins from Brookline, Newton, the affluent suburbs, shifted away, avoiding contact over the bargain counters, at the department stores, Filene's, Jordan. The crinkling of nostrils indicated their suspicion—South Boston was uninhabitable.

Doctor Please!

Had the rabbi appeared? Was it hallucination, a man in a torn black flannel suit floating above the synagogue chandeliers? Mass hysteria, a vision, prophecy? How about the cyclone—a natural disaster? Was he, Kezzlev, a victim of stomach upset, a glandular blip, a stem of *Amanita virosa* in the mushrooms capping a porterhouse steak that day at the Harvard Club, or a jealous colleague who had laced his sherry with lysergic acid? Polished pumps regaining the podium, Kezzlev remembered the lightness in his head, the crackling of white hairs in his scalp. What had *they* seen? Chochom Kezzlev went from door to door. Six hundred and thirty-nine members had been in the prayer hall with him. Questionnaires tucked under his arm, eighteen pages to be filled out in triplicate. The answers he hoped would give him some data, scientific basis to determine—what had happened?

Structure, diagrams, chart, training—all coming apart—each day he was more and more desperate to believe. Cycles, cross cycles, counter cycles, one inside another like an atlas of Ptolemy, celestial epicycles, tricycles, bicycles. He began to giggle as patients shut the door behind him, alone on his couch, cross cycle, icicle, lifecycle, popsicle? He bounded up and down on the thick foam rubber and sleek horsehide, thumb in his mouth. Mommy. Mommy. They believe me!

The phone was ringing, another patient. Can I help? Never have answers, but questions. Only one *he* wanted to ask, like his father Mendell, the Used Car Man, "Did *I* help?" Kezzlev in his swivel chair would suddenly be whirling around and round. Shock therapy? Existentialism? Theory—Jaspers—put yourself in a state of shipwreck. We'll both sail off the couch. *Maidelle*, let's try.

Women, men, came to him for witchcraft. Nothing too bizarre for the bored. The crazy—he got out a pill box and drugged them like elephants. Their monologues drove him round and round. He wanted to hop off, ask, he couldn't. He was frantic. Did I *help*? Did I do *good*?

A witch doctor could operate. Take Moses, he cut off, mutilated, circumcised. There was something. After three years you could say, your foreskin, anyway, I took away. Feel better?

He, Kezzlev, should have gone to Africa, not Vienna. Didn't Moses marry a black woman; learn her tricks?

I could put a bone in your nose, stretch a lower lip, tattoo … the problem was evil. Anxiety, terror, death, how to ward it off? His best clients, Jews, were already circumcised. Partnership with plastic surgeon—you could treat young girls, older women, cutting noses, taking bumps out, almost working wonders. Remove the clitoris? A testicle? What other parts could human beings spare—half a buttock to the gods, piece of an ear, toe? How could he help?

Jung, Freud, Adler, these men were intellectuals, talkers. Their techniques—the shock of talk—worked then but now? Everyone was wise, like some poison bacteria taken in, the population became immune, resistant, developed taciturn strains. Human fear was devious. It was getting harder and harder to outwit. He had crawled back with his teachers into the mouth, come out the bunghole, gone up into the womb, shot down the pole of DNA, biology, genetics, fed all the facts into M.I.T.'s computers, dossiers on each patient and all it spit out was "cuckoo, cuckoo."

Chochom Kezzlev jumped off his couch. The phone was ringing. He could hear his next patient scratching and banging on the door, pulling on the knob. Jaw clamped tight, Kezzlev tried to get his thumb out from between his teeth. The suck made his eyes swim.

He ran over to the wall and pulled the development map out of its metal canister on the wall. Four young psychiatrists in his postgraduate seminar and a Tibetan monk had labored with the computer for ten years. It was only a preliminary outline for a more complex diagram of interrelationships of oral, anal, adolescent, adult and senescent cycles: one constellation of characteristics spinning into the next with side revolutions due to eccentricity, favorable and unfavorable environments, bad luck, happenstance, plotted in a series of closing loops. He had to stop work because of nervous breakdowns. The Tibetan tried to stab Chochom with a quill. Now, pulling the chart until a thin parchment rug crackled across the oriental in his office, the doctor caught a familiar curve; fingers tracing depression, deprivation, masturbation, ineptitude, nervousness, nonsense; almost to the edge where a wooden rod put an end to speculation. He was floating in the blank space of senescence but approaching a series of brilliant gold circles, bands within bands, he had never seen before. Had they fooled him? Inscribed the parchment with invisible ink that was now seeping to the surface? Kabbalists, Sufis, his graduate students, the Himalayan? Whose hand painted this blinding spot in the midst of a blanched universe?

Abruptly the map rolled back, snapping. Kezzlev tried to pull it down but the parchment jammed and he was too clumsy with his thumb in his mouth.

"Chochom! Chochom!" Nurse and patient were banging on the door. It had iron bolts, a combination lock on the inside known only to himself, and a solid steel core three-inches deep buried in the walnut shell. They had to break down the wall before they could get through his lintel.

Under his couch was a trap door. It led to a crawl space between the floors. The doctor threw questionnaires into his briefcase, gathering them at random from the glittering waves of documents across the oriental. Papers spilled over chairs, mounted in waves to closet shelves. Yesterday he had met the last member of the congregation, a madwoman who was in and out of the asylum at Mattapan. Her form was ripped and torn where fingernails had slashed it as they knelt on her lawn, filling the papers out together.

Chochom tugged at his thumb again. It wouldn't budge. Rummaging with a free hand among the drawers of his cabinet, wading back and forth, debris of broken hypodermics, wooden mallet, handcuffs, tattered straight jackets; he found an old elastic bandage, a roll of tape, diapers. Unwinding, winding, he bound up the rigid limb from his elbow, over the forearm, wrist, knuckles, fingernail, to the tip of his thumb locked inside his lip. A strap around his neck as if he had a broken arm, he pushed the couch away from the wall.

"Doctor Kezzlev. Kezzlev!" In the outer office, he heard the tread of heavy boots, the broad Boston accents of the fire department. Always afraid, that nurse of his, playing psychiatrist, imagining he was about to hang himself, cut his throat, or like his father, Mendell, run the exhaust pipe into the end of the weekly lot special, a '34 Chevrolet coupe, that had come back from six unhappy customers. A lemon, which Mendell had sunk a fortune in to fix, not a single bolt, screw, spring in the thing original, yet no matter how it purred out of the Grove Hill shop, lay dead in a dozen extremities in a back street of Dorchester a week or two later. Mendell's citrus, his *esrog*, his holy fruit. "Idols," the last customer warned him. "*Baaliim*, machines—you are fixing devils. A whole lot of clay men, *golim*, Mendelle. Get a horse!" the bearded rabbi of the Orthodox synagogue in Roxbury had counseled. "An army of Sabbath breakers, dumbwaiters—these things are not God's creatures. Don't trust."

The coroner ruled—"accident" because they found Mendell kneeling under the steering wheel with his head through a hole in the engine wall, fingers in two of the spark plug holes, the ends of them mangled in valve stems, searching the heart of the Chevrolet. Insurance sent his son to school to master the inscrutable machine of the body, brains. Chochom put his mouth to his patients', breathed in bad breath. That was a danger, intoxication, gas of their bowels hissing out their mouths. Jonathan Swift warned, "humors that concluding in the anus formed a fistula," could rise to the head and cause ... Humors, biles, anatomies. Chochom shook his crammed briefcase. Melancholy? Anxiety, angels, devils, bile, I have to sift this stuff. It's hot.

Every Jew had seen the same, the cure, he was sure! In his teeth, the thumb slipped a notch. Then, his jaws jammed down again.

The doctor was in the crawl space between the floors of his building on Marlborough Street, side-stroking forward with his free arm, the briefcase tied around his waist. Others had recorded this business before but who had documentation, i.e., to wit, witness *at Sinai we saw an unnatural pillar, fire and smoke, heard voices,* signed statements from fifteen plumbers, twenty real estate operators, forty-five lawyers, sixty medical practitioners, and an assortment of two hundred self-made merchants in wholesale and retail garment, hardware, novelty item, grocery, dry goods, not a bunch of ex-hod carriers, but every one a sober, respectable citizen with no known history of second sight; corroborated by *their wives*.

No one wanted to admit. He had to keep ringing doorbells, hide in lawn shrubbery, jump out and buttonhole one by one, husband and wife apart, *glatt kosher*. Every one wanted to forget. The temple under its new president, rabbi, took a vote not to talk, for the sake of the Name, not to shame.

Chochom whose articles were begged for by learned journals was barred from the temple bulletin. They threatened to revoke his membership. "Fill in," he begged, "fill in, that is all, no follow up, no talk, never again. I'm leaving, see, just fill in *now*, for me." The last lady chased him over the backyard fence, knife in hand, screaming, threatening, still, after the fifth time around the house, she slackened. Crafty, on his toes, he triumphed, got her to drop the carver, pick up a ball point pen, her teeth knocking like hooves in her head, fill in, fill in, here—have a pill—fill, fill.

They wouldn't lie. Why?

The thumb began to vibrate in his mouth. He set his teeth deeper in the flesh. For the first few weeks after the event, dizzy with answers, the ringing of voices still in his ear after the last patients departed the couch, he found himself floating. All the rabbi's books had been brought to the analyst on Marlborough Street. Following the notes, thumb marks on pages, stains in the margin, grease spots, footsteps before him, Chochom had hope of one last synthesis, Sigmund and *Shechinah*.

I mean what were all those *mensche*s in the Zohar up to but getting into bed with Momma? Call me the *Shechinah*, Mother Spirit, Prosperina, Momma, every Jew trying to become God, the Father. He had to keep warning, there's not room for you, sonny, Me, in the same universe. So for a few hours Chochom thought he was close, only it all glimmered away in broken tea cups, wife swapping. He woke up. Momma! Momma! I'm going crazy.

A voice boomed in the crawl space. "You jealous?"

The doctor struck out in the darkness, squirmed.

"Take over," whispered a deep echo. "I quit. No-body loves Me."

Nobody loves me, Momma used to sing, Chochom remembered. *Everybody hates me I'm going to eat some worms.* "Momma?" he cried.

Light streamed before him. He wiggled toward a rush of voices. Poked his head out of a ventilation grate, jumped down. The fall's bang was swallowed up in a clangor of axes, poles, the squeak of rubber coats. As Chochom stepped onto the sidewalk he saw the shiny red trucks of the fire department parked in front of his Marlborough Street entry. "I quit. That's it!"

A hiss escaped his buttocks. He was about to—. The thumb was choking him or he would have called to the firemen, "Hose me down!"

He ran for the trolley. He had to think. The stink—. Everyone on the crowded in-town tram shifted seats, pulled away.

The doctor hid his face between his thumb and fist. His cheeks were glowing. The old universe had blown up. The fragments of it were in his pants, dripping to the trolley floor, trailing behind him as he slouched into Park Street station, Washington, changing trains, standing as the elevated rattled over Dover. He couldn't sit. Quit!

Nitwit, a voice mocked. Chochom was in tears. He undid his belt. The weight pulled his trousers down. A car full of ladies from Forest Hills started screaming. Chochom reached below and pulled his pants up. His face flamed squinting into the afternoon sun setting. "It!" he shouted to the fiery red faces of the Irish matrons. "It."

His thumb had shot out of his mouth—Egleston Station. Luggage abandoned—he left the train.

"Ahhhh! he called into the cavernous space of the transit authority's hangar. "Ooooom!" Steel rafters rang with the echoes. The dispatcher and the bus drivers lolling around the change booth looked up in surprise. "Ahhhhh!"

"Cut it out!" barked the dispatcher. The nightlights in the station snapped on.

Hearing other voices, Chochom cleared his throat, filled his lungs, sang, "Ooooom! Ahhhhhh!"

Dispatcher, bus drivers, took a few menacing steps toward him, forefingers cocked.

The doctor bayed, leapt into the air, his britches slipping, "Ooooom! Ahhhhh!" rattling bus windows, nickels in the change booth, the glass panes through the vast station hall, skipping ahead of the unbelievers who had begun to chase him onto the sidewalk and down Seaver Street along Franklin Park. His nether parts *farkuhkt*, exposed, trumpets announced the advent of prophecy, horns of passing motorists honking at the half-naked man cantering by Temple Mishken Tefilla's massy pillars. Let loose from his momma, poppa, teachers, past, present, whole earth and they that dwell therein. Start again. Not me. I couldn't hold the fire. A spark or two, but you, rabbi, I'll announce, sing. "Ooooooom! Ahhhhhhh!" The stars were making song in his sockets. The moon throbbed in his throat. Momma, he called to the light of the North Star glimmering in the dusk. Make love to me. O Rise!

Around him screamed not one, two, three, but dozens, police cars, their sirens joined his voice, streams of them converging on the avenue as he rounded the corner of Seaver Street. A host of angels, detectives, all of Boston, in a hunt for Messiah? Kezzlev kicked his heels, leaping into the air.

Three Black boys scrambling down a puddingstone cliff ran across the sidewalk in the doctor's path. Their bodies were luminescent. Tears glutted his eyes in the starlight. "You see him?"

"Devil!" they squealed, scattering before him, into the jam of vehicles.

"Devil, devil," Kezzlev intoned, in pursuit. A paddy wagon stopped, its door swung open, blocking his way. Blue arms reached out to drag him in.

"He stinks," grumbled one.

"Devil," called Kezzlev into disgruntled faces.

"He's full of sh …" another said in surprise. "You see a cop?"

"One, two, three …" Kezzlev pointed to the rear seat, then the front, laughing.

The clubs came down, smacking at the doctor. Lights went on, off. He began to giggle as an outraged voice insisted, "Shut up you cruddy nut!"

"Me! Meeeeeeee!" The doctor lost hearing just as the officers discovered he was leaking on their shoes and trouser pants. They whacked at the grin his mouth was locked in with a few tentative smacks of their baton.

"Dump him in the Neponset!"

"He's for Mattapan," kinder counsel intervened. Suddenly the smell thickened. Up front, the driver coughing, shouted over his shoulder, "Out!" The rear door swung open and they pushed the prophet from his fiery chamber.

Find a file in Forest Hills?

Five dollars for half a page!
Send first sentence to
Farmisht & Farblondgen
c/o This Paper.

Hospital Case

He awoke on a hospital bed, its starched white sheet patched in three places.

An old lady sat by his bed surrounded by shopping bags. She rocked back and forth humming, drawing up bruised half-eaten bananas, their gold skins like folded stars secured by rubber bands against spoiling; quarters of oranges, tangerines wrapped in torn cellophane. Occasionally, she plucked a vegetable from a bag, unwrapping radishes, carrots, a parsnip from individual pouches of brown paper.

Who? Where? How? A baby, he opened eyes on the world.

The lady bent over and pinched his cheek. "One month you were here, two," she whispered.

"Who?" he smiled, delighting her with the hoot that came out of his mouth.

"I'm not telling," the woman winked. She offered a banana.

"Who?"

The banana dripped in sweet mush over the patient's extended fingers. He licked them, sucked a wad of soft goo from his thumb. "Doctors," the lady continued. "Police, nobody."

A howl from the next bed shook the ward from one end to the other. "Nobody," boomed a voice. "I'm the Monkey Man."

"You got to whisper," said the lady. She twirled a finger at her ear. "*Meshuggeh.*"

"Who?" the patient asked again.

"Here? Everyone. Listen." In the next bed where the voice had boomed they could hear the springs creaking up and down as its Atlas, bronze from the sun, jumped on his mattress, calling, "Monkey! Monkey! Monkey!" Tattoos covered his body, cats, dogs, horses; on his chest, an ape, monkeys down his shoulders, all of whom he made wiggle and writhe as he knotted his sinews.

On the other side of them, a cadaver began to laugh in short soprano peals; music that set the whole room into chatter, seventy patients giggling at once. "Stop it!" screamed a nurse appearing out of a corridor. Keys jingling, the iron cage swung open and she rushed toward a corner where the attendant, chair slumped against the wall, snored with his hand in an open fly. "Hurry!" she shouted, slapping her assistant in the face. The two flew across the room, stripping a sheet from an abandoned bed—stuffing it in the cadaver's mouth—too late. A smell rose from the floor of the long room. The ward unstrung—pitch of the silver skull's cackle, loosening—.

"I got to go. Excuse me," the woman seated by his bed rose, leaving her shopping bags. "Watch," she called as she lumbered through the unlocked door of the ward, pointing to her paper trunks. The nurse hurried after the shopping lady, whines of "Mommy! Mommy!" rising on all sides.

"Who?" the patient kept repeating until his companion returned. "Who?"

"For a month you were in special therapy; new sheets, blankets, doctors three times a day. After they brought you in, you slept, slept and slept. So now, a month, you're here. I didn't say anything. I'm thinking, a rest. Sleep. Forty days, nights, a few more. Once they find out, a fuss, *gantsa machiah*, noise, hullabaloo, who's who, what's what, where's where, you'll never get nothing straight. *Nu?*"

"*Nu?*" the patient nodded.

The lady straightened her bags, put her hand deep in one to the side of her paper bins, creases mottled with spots and drew out a herring. In a collapsible cupboard to the left, she rooted with her fingers until she located a container of sour cream, the bottom of which she scraped with a ragged rubber spatula until a spoonful accumulated which she dropped on the fish laid out in her lap on wax paper.

"Doctor," she whispered, slicing a piece off the herring's tailbone, ladling it into his mouth with the spatula. "I heard you."

"*Nu?*"

"All the way from Egleston Station I followed. You couldn't hear. Honking. Seven bags. I was tied down."

Blue shadows began to fill the patient's head, the faint far away sound of horns, a patter of sticks on his brain. His eyebrows came together in a furrow.

At the threshold of memory, he raised his hand, brushing the past away, "*Nu?*"

"I saw them. But what could I do, scream, help? Bums, no-goods, *nu* can you sue? *Norishkeit*! Worse for you." The lady leaned over the bed, caught the doctor's hand in the air. She pressed it between her plump pink palms, lacy with wrinkles. "What they did to you smacking … whacking … *gazloniim, chazurrim*, what they did to your thumb."

"Who?"

"Monkey! Monkey!" The man in the bed on the right began to jump up and down. The doctor started to cry. Salty tears caught in the bristle of his badly shaved face. Gold streaks of sun ran down the dirty windows.

"To chew on you. Beasts! *Vilde menschen*!" She cradled the hand against her cheek, one whose thumb had been sown back on at Mattapan State, crooked, a bit to the left.

The cadaver's face in the bed on his left nodded to him, shaking a mouth stuffed with rags. Every ridge and depression of cheek, chin bone outlined, skin like wax paper drawn tight over an outcropping of skull. The Monkey Man on the right, thundered, squatted, rolled the animals on his arms in coils of muscles. The woman surrounded by her bags was telling a story.

A hand drew an outline in the darkness. A first point of light, and from that streamed another, lesser light. The farthest dying rays of that effulgence furnished the fundament for a further palace out of which burst broad avenues of silver and gold and broke the dam of senselessness in the patient's own eyes, ears, nose. He heard. "Doctor!" He was a doctor. He understood, staring at her, stationed between mercy, stern judgment.

"Who?" he asked.

"A doctor," she replied.

"Doctor who?"

"Shhhhh …" she whispered. Around them a room full of fragments groaned. What good were pieces of a former life? The dry skin of the snake lay on the asphalt entrance to the park. Her long dead father, a cough hacking at his consonants, spoke of ancients who joined letter to letter, searching for the hidden universe, a house of high doors shut against unbelievers. His dreams danced now from the dust of a kitchen on Kingsdale Street to the hospital. They lit walls smeared with excrement, corners clotted with spider webs, garbage underfoot, spilled soups and crusts, noodles, pecked at by skeletal pigeons, flapping arms and legs in white underwear who crawled along the floor, the nurses sunk in torpor.

Mummies rustled in their sheets—silver light spread from the shopping bags to soften their features. The tale of Laban the Syrian, Jacob's uncle, idols gibbering in his ears; of *Shechinah*, that presence come down to man, lady *K'fillah*, the covering, sucking at his seed, bright beads—strung on the shaft from the first flash through the dross of the universe, irradiated world after world. Time flashes in and out of existence.

• • •

Outside in the night draped over Mattapan, Roxbury, Jamaica Plain, a fold of the moon falls. The bricks of the ward glow to the rush of wings. For the guard, bleary eyed with drink it is a sudden wind. He looks through the bars of the window. Inside, everyone lies fast asleep, even the attendants. Reaching out to touch the sterling shimmer of the building, his fingers burn and breaking the pint of whiskey in his rear pocket, he falls back into weeds, a fang between his legs.

Inside they see the tree, its branches poke up through the plastic tiles of the floor, the shaft pierce the roof. Starlight floods down.

The Monkey Man has washed out of his flesh idolatry of animals and is speaking of Behemoth, Leviathan. He who denied the resurrection of the body, the cadaver, clapped "our bones are dried, our hope lost," clinging to his sockets, receives Ezekiel's assurance. Eden wafts through his sinus. The lady of the bags reclines before the doctor, flirts with angels, persistent *ophanim* pinch her sunburned cheek. They are to be gathered up in folds of psalms. All who have been entangled with mothers, fathers, children, unable to unwind from forbidden dreams, tied into knots, shrunken into orifices, mouths, anuses: caught in the shadows of the tree's roots, thick loops—loosed of unnatural bonds, begin to climb and rise toward the light.

"Messiah!" Sparks lodged in their throats stream up.

"Maishe," cries the lady. "Maishe!"

The patient sees in the air above his head, not in a clap of thunder and whirlwind, falling bricks, scraps of prayer book, but illuminated, the face of Maishe Ostropol. Stretching his limbs the patient catches an outstretched arm.

The others float below, as the patient is borne upward on purple waves, grapes pressed between his lips. The ward feeds on the clusters falling greedily, nectar running down their chins. "Maishe," he cries. The latter's fingers grasp his in a flood of dark, dizzy liquor.

Young Man Messiah

Rochelle slumped in the back seat of a deserted synagogue—but she has flitted out of the body. A spark, from the cobwebs of the ceiling lights her back to the time when she was a teenager.

Her feet tap the polished slats, upstairs at the YM-HA's hall on Seaver Street in white bobby socks and short skirt spun around the crowded dance floor by a tall guy in loafers, black flannel slacks, camel's hair jacket. "Sammy Schwartz!" the boy shouts his name, showing off skills in rhythm and blues, standing on one foot, moving his other, smiling like a ballroom impresario. Rochelle whirls back and forth, paying no attention as Sammy attempts to lead or follow. That is when she sees Sammy's friend. From the wall in a press of unhappy looking boys, this guy glares over the dance floor at her schoolmates; girls from Dorchester, Mattapan, Roxbury, whose parents let them take the trolley or walk over to the Young Man's Hebrew Association. The mothers chaperoning the dance aren't happy about Schwartz or the other older boys with him. This is a

Junior High School Hop. By the wall, the guy who keeps staring makes no motion toward anyone. When Rochelle catches his eye, he begins to scratch his face.

It is awful what he is doing to himself. By the end of the evening, his face is bleeding. She wonders why he keeps looking at her. Afterwards, her friends consent to let Schwartz and four of his friends walk them back to their streets. Rochelle thinks of saying something to the guy with the bloody face, but he is hanging behind. Schwartz is pestering her with jokes and cute talk. She knows he is going to ask for a date, the next weekend. Her mother has told her, strictly no, no, no.

Anyway, these guys are too old for her or her friends. There are three years between them. Schwartz and his gang don't belong at the dance, which is for eighth and ninth graders. These boys are sixteen, almost seventeen, almost in college. There is something wrong when they have to show up at a party for younger kids. Rochelle and her friends are just past thirteen, though Sandy's breasts are bigger than most of their mothers'. Rochelle's are already showing. She has to slap the boys' hands away; watch her brother's funny stuff. He pretends to come close for a hug. Schwartz is talking about a car ride and a movie—would she like to go out to a restaurant? He is cute, tall, very black hair, a nice looking long tweed coat, red woolen scarf, like a college boy. He tries to pull her in and reach his hand around her coat and touch … "What are you stupid?"

She pushes Schwartz away with the shout. He spoiled it. Sandy is giggling up ahead. Some guy named Donny has his arm around her, talking a mile a minute and hugging her closer and closer as they walk. "Look seriously," the Sammy character was saying, his cheeks red, trying to catch up with Rochelle as she walked faster. If she had to, she was going to run home ahead of them all and let Sandy and Margie take care of themselves. "Why don't we see a movie together."

"I'm busy," Rochelle snapped.

"The week after," Schwartz persisted.

"I'm busy."

"The middle of the week?"

"I'm busy."

Schwartz gave up and fell back to the three or four characters trailing behind the two guys, talking to Sandy and Margie. That's when the one with the bleeding face came up. Rochelle was afraid to look at him.

He was almost at her ear, however, and he whispered, "*Raub dir das Weib, für das dein Herze fühlt!'—So denkt der Mann: das Weib raubt nicht, es stiehlt.*" It sounded in her earlobe like her mother's Yiddish, though the syllables were harsher. His voice was deep and hoarse.

She should just walk faster, but Rochelle turned towards him, staring at his feet, and asked, "What does it mean?"

"Grab the woman, for whom your heart feels. So thinks the man, the woman doesn't grab, she steals."

"What's the matter with you?" Her tone was not as sharp as it could have been.

"'Double pain is lighter to bear, than single.'" The breath from his lips was close to her nose. "'Accept a dare!'"

She glanced at his face, a sneer creeping into his mouth, and snaking through the cheeks where marks of his fingernails could still be seen in long red welts. She stopped walking to look at him. He winced at her stare but she also found his black eyes fixed on her, attractive. "What do you want?"

He didn't say anything but his fingers went to his face again. A lump that he worried on his chin began to bleed.

"Why are you hurting yourself?"

"'I am wrapping the cloak of the sublime around the ugly,'" he snapped, taking his hand away.

"You're not so ugly."

"Where do you live?"

Rochelle told him and he asked if she wanted him to walk her home. "If you want to," she answered and it came out a bit more flip than she intended. He frightened her. He was too old but his eyes were sort of crazy in a way that made her want to stare back. They walked on in silence for a block. Sammy Schwartz was talking to one of her girlfriends with the other guys. She waved good-bye to them as they turned to the left. "What's your name?"

"Maishe."

"I mean your real name."

"I told you."

"That's your Jewish name."

"It's my real name."

"You are strange."

"Do I scare you?"

"I don't know …" They were turning up her block and she had to get rid of him before the front steps where her mother would be waiting, ready with a million questions. "Why don't you …?"

But Maishe broke in again. "Do you want to go out?"

"Sure." She didn't know if she meant it. He was fumbling around in his coat pocket for a pencil.

"Let me have your number."

She gave it to him and whispered, "Why don't you leave me here. It's better."

"I'll call," he shouted as she skipped away toward her front door.

He was too old, but she wasn't going to tell her mother. "So what happened? What happened?" They two of them must have been standing, waiting for her in the front hall an hour already. It was only 10 P.M., and the dance was going on for another half hour already. "You said nine thirty. Nine thirty, Rochelle!" her mother cried.

"I don't know. I don't know," her father was mumbling.

"What don't you know," she said giving her mother a quick peck on the cheek.

"If I can trust. If I can trust you."

"Don't," she snapped, breaking away, heading for her room.

"And what does that mean? What does that *mean*—Rochelle?" asked her father, running after her. Her mother's scream was muffled. Rochelle had gotten to the bedroom first and slid the bolt behind her.

"At least talk to me. Talk to me, Rochelle. Princess, talk!" her father pleaded.

"Oy vey," she sighed aloud. Over and over, every day! What did her parents want? She should grow up or not?

• • •

"Who's this?" her mother was hissing. "A boy, he sounds too old. Is he in your class?" It was Maishe on the phone. He had his father's car. Did she want to go to a movie?

"Yes, yes," she screamed into the phone. "I'll meet you on the corner."

"What corner—what is this with corners?" her mother was asking.

"I can't," Rochelle said, when he asked if she could talk.

"All right, the corner, Woodrow and Blue Hill, Saturday, Seven-thirty," he repeated, to confirm her accepting his suggestion.

"Fine, fine," she assented and hung up.

"What's going on?" her father intoned dramatically at the table. Her idiot older brother was smirking. "Who is this calling?"

"A kid from school," Rochelle answered.

"So what is this corner business."

"I'm going for an ice cream."

"Alone?"

"I need a chaperone for a chocolate cone?"

"He can't come to the house? Sit down! Your mother can't give you a dish, a pint, a quart of ice cream in the kitchen—you have to sneak to corners."

"Everybody meets on the corner there."

"Who is everybody?" her father wanted to know.

"Sandy … Margie …"

"Oh, that Sandy with the big blouse. Already that one is acting too big for her britches," said her mother.

"What do you mean?"

Her brother sniggered in the corner of the kitchen. "Your brother," her mother began, then broke off, seeing her daughter's face turning an angry purple and the lips of her small, dark mouth pressing tight together.

"I didn't …" he burst out.

"Let him tell you about himself," Rochelle shouted. "Let him tell you what he tried, when she came over, the last time, Sandy …"

"What night is the date?" said her father, cutting off the exchange before his wife who was eyeing her first born suspiciously could be thrown off the track. But his daughter was quicker than he was.

"Wednesday."

"A school night?"

"So, it's just a cone."

"No, absolutely, no."

She got up, left the table and slammed the door to her room while he followed behind after her, banging, "Don't you dare. Don't you dare!"

"Please. Sidney. She's still a baby. A baby. What are you doing?"

"Respect. I want respect. I got to have some more respect from this fresh little *pishekeh*. Respect, you hear? Rochelle, you can take it off."

"Stop it! Stop it!" Inside the bedroom, Rochelle relaxed. It was turning into the familiar fight about the brassiere and now her mother had changed sides and was calling her father names. "Are you crazy? Are you sick? Sidney!"

"Take it off."

"She has breasts. What's the matter with you? Stop it."

"Respect!"

• • •

On Saturday night, Rochelle walked past the Morton Street Theater and the double bill, half of which she was supposed to see with Margie. He was waiting, sitting in his car, an old Buick convertible. The leather smelled nice as she slipped in and waved good-bye to Margie who looked at her apprehensively, calling back, "Nine thirty, don't forget."

"Nine thirty?" he asked.

"I have to be careful. My parents don't know I'm going out."

"How old are you?"

"Do you care?" Rochelle asked.

He looked at her and they both laughed. It was the nicest moment of the evening. After that he started quoting people she had never heard of, on and on, all through the ride to Brookline, the meal in a fancy Chinese restaurant, the drive back, the parking lot in Franklin Park where he put his arm around her and started kissing.

She fought off his tongue but let his fingers creep under her blouse and into the cups of the brassiere. But it was impossible for him to wrestle her down so as to undo the clips. And when he tried to put his hand between her legs, she closed them and pushed back. "No."

"Why not?"

"I'm not ready."

"You feel ready."

"I'm not." He tried wrestling a few minutes more but she pushed his fingers out of her blouse as well, frightened. "I don't want to now." Suddenly, he jerked back up, took the wheel again, turning on the ignition, backing out of the parking lot, and started home again, exiting right from Franklin Park down Blue Hill Avenue. "Oh my God!"

Her watch—straightening herself out, beside him, she glanced at her wrist by the glow of the speedometer—it read ten thirty.

"They're going to kill me," Rochelle said.

"What's the matter?"

"My parents."

"I'll take you to the door and explain."

"No, no. Stop at Woodrow Ave. and see if Margie is still there."

Margie wasn't there. But Rochelle recognized her father in the brand new black Oldsmobile, parked ominously a few car lengths from the corner. She ducked just in time. "Oh my God!"

"What is it?"

"My father."

"So?"

"He's crazy. Look, take me to a telephone booth … Just wait." She scrambled out a few blocks on down Morton and called Margie. Coming back to the car, she said, "Drop me on Callendar Street." They backtracked.

"What happened?"

"Margie will make up a story. We got lost in the movies. I thought she stayed to see the second feature. I called and I'm walking over to her house for my father to pick me up. You let me off a few houses down."

"Shall I call?"

"I don't know."

"Why not?"

"Okay, but call around four in the afternoon, next Thursday."

When he telephoned, she told him bluntly. "You are too old for me."

"What do you mean?" Maishe asked.

She added in a slightly more apologetic tone. "My mother doesn't want me to go out."

"Did they find out?"

"Sort of. It's too much trouble."

"'*Wie komm ich am besten den Berg hinan?*'—*Steig nur hinauf und denk nicht dran!*'"

"What does that mean?" Rochelle asked, irritated.

"It's Nietzsche."

"Who is he?"

"A man who died of syphilis."

She let him breathe heavily for a moment or two into a silent black receiver before she spoke, sadly. "I'm only thirteen." He was about to reply when she heard a key in the lock of the front door, "Oh God, it's my mother. I have to hang up."

It was four years later before Rochelle saw him again, a mixer at Harvard Hillel in Cambridge. She had let a friend drag her from the freshman dormitories at Boston University to see if they could meet some interesting boys. He was dressed in a three-piece suit with a silver key chain across his tummy, a heavy blue coat with a fur collar thrown over his shoulders and a bowler hat. The other boys in the crowd that spilled out of the doorway on Bryant Street into the front yard and street were in blue blazers or tweed sport coats. He was standing at the fence on the sidewalk in front of the rambling stucco mansion where the dance was being held. Was he at the mixer or not? There were nothing but jerks at the Hillel dance, too many freshman boys, a glut of sophomores with slumped shoulders and bent spines, a few graduate students who hadn't been able to find a girl either in college or afterwards. She even spotted one or two of the sad sacks from the G&G Delicatessen on Blue Hill; guys who dropped out of night school—desperate to meet anyone. She was sure it was him, although there weren't as many red blotches on the face and his hair was much longer. The way he eyed the girls coming in and out of the gateposts like Count Dracula was the clincher.

"Are you Maishe Ostropol?"

"Who are you?" he said, surprised, a blush spreading through his face because he had been staring at her, not expecting to be recognized.

"You took me out once."

He didn't answer but stared harder.

"You don't remember?" Rochelle asked.

"I did? How could I forget you?" He asked it as if he wasn't trying to be funny.

"You were too old for me," Rochelle replied.

He looked into her eyes. His were as black as her own. She felt her cheeks flush in the cold November weather. Both of them laughed, as he asked, "Am I too old now?"

"No." Without thinking she had answered and now he put his arm through her own and took her off for a drink in his rooms.

It all happened quickly, too quickly, she told herself afterwards. Because he understood she loved him and he could not really make sense of that; although it had been wonderful at first. "What were you doing there?" she asked, lying back naked on his bed.

"Like Kierkegaard, I was making a fool of myself in public."

"Why"

"To become aware of my own absurdity." She had read Kierkegaard, a few pages of him, on her own, but she didn't say anything. Instead, she came up and put her arms around him. He was cute when he looked a little scared. She pressed her small breasts against his shirt. Was he afraid of what might happen? The thick red oriental rug in his room, the rows of books on the shelves, the fire he had lit and the whiskey they both had drunk over the last few hours made her drowsy and contented. She didn't feel the least bit absurd. She began taking his clothes off too, giggling at his sudden reticence. "When do you have to leave?" he whispered.

"Midnight."

And a while later … "Did you ever …"

"Once … almost."

• • •

Was it a mistake? Should she have kept at a distance? Made him crazy?

After they got married he tried teaching in Boston, a year at the law school, then the rabbinical seminary. He was so passive it was hard to predict what happened. Soon she couldn't understand a word he was saying and she suspected under it, he didn't like her anymore. Her parents were happy at last. Her friends full of envy, such a big house, a swimming pool, a rabbi, a fancy new car, and how about children?

And he wouldn't speak to her about it. He wasn't sleeping in the same bed anymore. Instead he talked about angels and stayed out late at night. He talked to the young women in his synagogue and had them over at all hours of the night, as if he were a doctor. When she tried to discuss their problem, suggest they see a psychiatrist, a marriage counselor, another rabbi, he laughed. "Better, look at a reading list."

"Some things aren't in books," she protested.

"What?"

"Me."

That was the time he told her, "If you had let me when we first met, we might have entered together, we might have gone through the gates."

"The gates?"

He looked away. He did it when he felt he was not being understood and it had turned into a habitual gesture when he was with her. "I was thirteen," she said, trying to apologize.

He looked up suddenly, his eyes moist, "Yes."

"Thirteen?"

And then he looked away and she had lost him.

The Last of the Ponkapoags

The last Ponkapoag in Boston Bay, Chickatabot, knelt in the shadow of a lump of puddingstone where he had pitched his spring camp. He was rubbing two damp sticks together. The rain had soaked into his blanket, moccasins and skin tent. His leggings were moldy with mud from the Neponset River, where his wife last week was dumped.

Six days of drizzle. He sniffed, blew his nose in a brittle brown oak leaf, hoping he wouldn't come down with plague, playing with fire. He thought, must be an easier way to do this, catch, catch! He had cornmeal, spring water, a pheasant he had shot with bow as it sprang out of the nearby grass. Roasting its breast, chewing oily bird bones, the thought quickened forefingers, thumbs, so the sticks whirled with a knack he imagined lost and, into dry bits of tinder spilled underneath, a tiny dart of fire spun. Blowing, blowing, feeding it with scraps of *The Boston Globe, Herald American*, his eyes swum with tears for the spirit watching over him, the first blush of warmth in his bones since the blaze had guttered out last night in a gust of wind and water.

"Stupid," he grunted. "You ain't no Sioux." He needed birch bark, saplings, a regular lodge like his great-great-great-grandfather Cutshumaquin. This sticky weather was the same. Still, he had to be careful. Squatting was tricky. If he could stay put, say, seven years, there was no way they could shove him off. He had a stone hatchet to scare juveniles, fishing line for Scarboro Pond, rabbit traps, and his heart was set on a fox skin by summer.

Chickatabot smiled. Despite the sniffle he was in good shape. Social Security would see him through the first season. Chives in the long brown grass of the unmown meadows by Hagborne Hill spiced his pheasant, wild onions.

Since the policeman had been shot, the park was a no-man's-land. Chickatabot's family had been coveting this spot, since they moved away eleven generations before. The original Chickatabot's son, Josiah, signed, shifted off, just to be friendly. "Why not?" The White boys would stay a season, move on. There were greener pastures just beyond. The Ponkapoags took a few buckets of beads, gewgaws, buttons, as a token of gratitude. Go ahead, sit, sit, no inconvenience, nice here, huh?

Where they all came from? The Ponkapoags could never figure. Elbowed out of Roxbury, Mattapan, Milton, his great-great-grandfather Moho had got fed up at the last remove—taxes, rents, the reservation closed—and had gone into hiding. Never pay, the Moho family whoop, circling Boston Bay, sitting in wasteland, dump-land, salt marsh, swamp, sneaking back to the Neponset, now dirty as dishwater, under bridges, subway lines, to sing their dirges; more difficult as the family decreased.

To keep the Massachusetts blood running clear! The relatives on Martha's Vineyard, wary, turned up their noses the last hundred years. He had to sneak up North for his own wife, not even the Passamaquoddy were taking. They had heard about the down and out Mohos, scrounging garbage cans, the White man's backyard, couldn't understand what it was all about. Chickatabot slipped under the fence at the border, kept on until New Brunswick where he found a bride, fat, oily, with big eyes when he spun a story out—city life, Scollay Square, the bright lights. Boston! Ha, screaming, he had to give her a few knocks when she saw his Canton shack and lean-to.

Coon pie, squirrel, brown rabbit stew, Chickatabot's mouth watered—bachelor life! That squaw had not stopped from the day she squatted down on the three-legged stool in the shack, grunted at the furniture, vegetable garden, squawking. Cans of food she wanted, a car, refrigerator, electricity, radio, a Micmac. Crazy for civilization! He spat, but went out snooping, yard-to-yard, until the town constable got wind of the junk collecting in Chickatabot's back lot, kicked them out. "Last of the Mohos" he declaimed, showing up at town meeting. "You do this to last of Moho, curse come on Canton." But the Yankees, who threw a crumb his family's way, were dying out. Irish, Jews, Poles had pushed into Canton's woods around the ponds. Chickatabot in the twentieth century was a public nuisance; town cops looked the other way but neighbors sent state troopers in to dispossess his spot not far from the old Ponkapoag reservation. Tall police in blue breeches and boots, they shooed him away from the split-levels springing up on Neponset hunting grounds. All that squaw's fault! Sticking to squash, pumpkin, corn, he was a curiosity.

Three hundred pounds of nagging on his back, Chickatabot shuffled through neighboring Dedham, Stoughton, Easton. For a while they slept in an abandoned boxcar on a siding in Sharon among the Neponset swamps to the cry of the *New York, New Haven* whistles; locomotives pounding down the line. She boiled duck soup from the canvasbacks he caught springing in the waterlogged morass with a plate of wild cranberries, water lily, salads and fruits. In leggings smeared with axle grease, mink and beaver oils, he skimmed the flooded fields with a dugout canoe, a log, he burnt and hatcheted to shape, poling up the Neponset, sliding through the pipe at its junction with the Charles, snagging trout in their upper branches, bream, a batch for freshwater chowder. Even after the damming and scooping of the sewage systems, he knew every lump of the brackish bottoms in these southeastern Massachusetts ponds, streams, children of the Mother Brook drained away to a ghost. His stomach toughened to thick leather, soaked up mercury, DDT, no worse than tannic acid to a calfskin.

A trickle of water wet the corner of Chickatabot's cheek. Halcyon, sitting in the sun outside the boxcar, waving at the passengers speeding between metropolises, golden pickerels frying in the pan, scales radiant, a glint like mallard's feathers below his nose while the wife puttered about the pots steaming sassafras. Trading fur skins with a furrier in Randolph for nickels, dimes and dollars, buying bangles for the squaw.

One night, in the shadow of the Blue Hill, as if a mountain of granite, clay, mud, wood had crashed into them, the boxcar was slammed, its wheels began to squeal as they sat up on their straw beds. Before they could get to the door, their house was moving, chugging along—just enough time to slide open the panel and jump.

Railroad dicks laughed at them, shaking six shooters, get a move on it, giving his squaw the eye.

He had only to fade back into the underbrush, throw up another shack in Stoughton, but the wife was lonely for people, faces in the window a few times a day. Through cursing, shouting, she wept, until his fish, squirrel, had no taste. The dish of wild strawberries wilted, washed in her bitter eyes. The poles of the lean-to folded, he scrounged with her toward backyards again, East Dedham, Westwood, Mattapan, Braintree. Chickatabot stole from trashcans, spread blankets in deserted houses, cellar holes. One winter he bedded down in a Nantasket summer cottage boarded up, burning knickknacks in the fireplace to keep warm until a passing patrol car saw the smoke late one night and stopped.

He squinted into flashlights while his wife smiled. Warm cell, three meals a day, something to look forward to, he whispered in pigeon Algonquin as the squad car pulled away, electricity shut off in the Nantasket house, think of all the bright lights.

• • •

"What were you doing?" the judge asked him, snapping, a skinny man with a shock of white hair.

Chickatabot shook his head.

"What were you doing in that house?" the judge repeated shrilly.

"Sittin'," mumbled Chickatabot.

"Squattin'?" asked the judge, cupping his ear. "Did you say squattin'?"

The Indian nodded.

"Mr. Moho," said the justice, "You and your … " his finger went round in little circles in the air, "*woman*, have a list of arrests for vagrancy and trespassing as long as the Neponset. You usually confine yourself to the tributaries of that river, its trunk and drainage system. Now, you suddenly show up in Nantasket, attracted by the roar of breakers, salt spray, clement air, numerous opportunities in its sparsely populated streets during the winter season to squat? Aye?"

Chickatabot nodded.

"Mr. Moho, this nation was founded by squatters. Not an inch of American soil, title to which was not cemented by some form of squat. However," he shook his finger in the Indian's face, "There are rules. The squat that establishes title must take place on a spot of land unoccupied by other bottoms. In the course of squatting, Mr. Moho, you committed crimes and misdemeanors in the Commonwealth. Breaking. Entering. Vandalizing. I have here a tearful letter from Mr. & Mrs. Chaim Wyzanski, who regret their inability to appear in person, stating that you consigned to fire a stock of valuables and irreplaceable souvenirs, collected through seven years of winter vacations in St. Petersburg, Florida: two dozen leather alligators, a box of hand-carved coconuts, ebony statuary without number, a gross of Kewpie dolls, stuffed teddy bears, memorabilia of three decades, assorted museum-worthy sundries: moreover that you soiled sheets, blankets, articles of underwear: and your 'companion' Mrs. Moho, is suspected to harbor about her person six to eight shifts and petticoats of the Seminole Nation.

"Gentlemen," said the Judge, looking up at the arresting officers, clerk of court, and recording secretary. "There are conflicting claims here. The defendant appears without benefit of counsel. There is some legal basis for his assertion of simply exercising his right to squat. He chose to visit us despite wintry gales and snowy hillocks, here on the salt sea's marge; and those Wyzanskis were loathe to interrupt their warm vacation further in order to testify today, I see a way we may adjudicate this nicely. Hem!

"Moho, have you ever held a job?"

"No," whispered Chickatabot, trembling. He heard a devil in the judge's voice. It was the end—the last of the Ponkapoag.

• • •

It was not the seven years suspended sentence that crushed Chickatabot. It was the marriage certificate.

• • •

The judge began to pull out the drawers of his desk. In one hand he held a Bible, in the other a whiskey bottle. "Take it like a man," he advised, draining a third of the bourbon before passing it to the newlyweds. He called Sanitation in Boston—an old crony there from his days on the governor's council, and Chickatabot was set shoveling for life.

The squaw was radiant, hauling her inebriated husband first to a halfway house on Columbus Avenue, then to a flat nearby. He rose in a haze for the next fourteen years, no worse than the rest of the crew, Irish, Italian, hauling garbage.

The Ponkapoag's eyes were dizzy after his meager pickings in suburban towns, Milton, Stoughton, Weymouth, at the swill Bostonians threw away: bags of edibles, boxes of usables. Astonished, he tried the first few days to take it home but the malice of his fellows made Chickatabot turn the thing into a joke. Swaying, he tossed the burlap bag in which halves of grapefruit, orange quarters, a radio, ham bone, a pair of pants and assorted costume jewelry were collected back into the grinding maw of the disposal unit. "Just foolin'," he grumbled as they toasted the "Portugee" with a pint of Three Roses, its bouquet rising over the crushed fruits and vegetables his clothes were fetid with.

He forced cheap wine and rye down, fourteen years of fiery water, burning it up, smoking his eyes, nose, mouth so he couldn't taste, smell, see. He pushed out the door each morning, shoveled, was spat out of the back of the truck at night to fall into his partner's arms. Floating in fumes one day his legs began to shiver and the barrel started shaking in all directions, splattering the crew—he couldn't stop. Devils, demons were shouting, chopping, whole headdresses of turkey feathers, clam shells, bird nests, beaver burrows, chewed up in the jaws he was feeding them, flocks of wild duck, deer herds, horns, antlers, all chawing, chawing, schools of herring, bream, lobsters, mussels, grass, trees. Chickatabot screaming—dove into the metal jaws to stop it. Just in time they stopped the truck.

Two weeks later, dried out, a wraith, he limped home to the squaw, a glint in his eye.

He was retired.

"Retired?" She shook her head, making no sense of it. He muttered a few words in Algonquin. Then he walked over and—to be sure she understood—slammed her.

He pulled the telephone out of the wall by the cord and wound the black line around her neck. He grinned and gave it a slight tug.

The squaw sat in a corner whimpering. He coiled electric cord around her tummy, toes, thumbs, waiting for midnight.

At twelve o'clock he set his house on fire.

Gagged and trussed, he slung her over his shoulder, stood in the narrow backyard singing songs until he heard the fire engine's sirens.

Shifting his squaw's weight, he started to hotfoot it through the lanes and alleys of the South End, sure of himself. He knew a street in Roxbury where police were afraid to come. Garbage disposal shot through as fast as they could and no other city services had been near for years. There was an abandoned garden shack just right for him behind a burned out wooden mansion whose charred bulk blocked any scrutiny from passing cars.

He cautioned his wife not to talk to the neighbors. Slurring his voice, he said he was from the South. They were not friendly to red folk. One family of Micmac who had come down to settle were driven out of Roxbury on short notice. Only the squaw said nothing. She had sat in the corner since their removal from the South End, silent. "You sick?" he asked, setting a meal he had scraped together out of ash cans a few blocks away.

Her face was shrinking. He wanted to get back to Stoughton, Canton, but she was too weak to move. He set out to scout there alone and came back, sadly. Row after row of neat bungalows, two bedroom frames, backed into the woods he remembered—impossible to make a camp. Scuffing his moccasins on the broken sidewalks across Hyde Park where he had abandoned the Mother Brook and a raft he had tied together, Chickatabot slunk into West Roxbury, trying to find a shortcut through the few green spaces, clumps of trees, left in Boston: golf courses, cemeteries; padding out of the Mount Hope graveyard into the Forest Hills burial grounds, his nose quickened. Ahead of him he smelled rabbit. He began to trot in the direction of the scent and was soon zigzagging after shadows, leaping stone markers, toward Morton Street, hopping the rock wall into Franklin Park. Cottontails scattered in all directions as he ran through the tall, uncut grass, milkweed. A covey of grouse burst from their winter straw, drumming their wings. Raccoons swarmed everywhere, thickets furry with tails. Trees, bushes, lawn, stretched in unbroken soft green and brown as far as he could see, acres of wild land teeming with game. Why not? he thought. He could squat.

Hurrying home to Roxbury, he slammed the door of the shack behind him. "Come on," he shouted. "We got fresh air. Good hunting. Sweet water."

The squaw did not stir.

Chickatabot was rifling the drawers in the bureau for cash. He dragged a leather bag out, threw pots, pans, a wooden plate into the satchel. "You coming?"

The woman's head hung down on her chest.

"You smell bad." Chickatabot sniffed the air.

She didn't answer.

He walked over and tugged her braid of black hair. "You hear?" The squaw tumbled out of the chair. The crack of her bones broke the stillness. Her body rocked on the planks. Leaning down, he touched her—stiff as a bird.

He swallowed; stuffed her in the leather bag, pulled the drawstrings tight and sat down to cry. It was mean, he wailed; mean to take away his love just when he needed her. How could he settle in the park alone, hey, hey? He kept up the dirge until he heard the neighbors shouting, "Shut up!" through their windows.

Chickatabot rose, wiped his eyes—time later for the long lament to marsh grass and sea gulls at the Neponset. He cut poles from the trees in the backyard that night and tied them together with twine, slinging a moth-eaten deerskin between the canes to form a sledge. Roping his baggage in, he set off by moonlight for the river.

Now, a week after the funeral rites, miraculously fire caught in the wet twigs cradled in the puddingstone. Flames crackled about Chickatabot's head. Showers of sparks snapped at his feet, elbows, as the wet beech logs sizzled in the heat of the blaze and spat out water and steam. In the mist, a figure loomed, a small, fat woman like his wife. Only he had weighted his wife down with rocks, broken crockery, a granite boulder, lashed as ballast into the sledge. Her wasted bulk was too slight to carry her under and the poles, skin, corpse floated on the oily Neponset water that came trickling in long cold fingers through the brown mat of weeds swamped in the spring flood. Embracing stones, her cheek against the pillow of a rusting tire hub, his woman had finally sunk as he pushed the muddy bier out a second time into the middle of the current and watched the waters swallow it up. Shivering on the shore, up to his ankles in black ooze, he sang to the squaw all the songs his grandfather had taught him until the first faint light of dawn spread across the Atlantic horizon.

So now the shape in Franklin Park took him by surprise, silver in the fog and rain. Looking up he saw a woman's arm shake. A shining bright knife cut across his copper cheek as she screamed, "I'll kill him."

Mirl's Mother Loose

"I'll kill him. Don't tell me. Everyone told me. He's here. Hiding. Tapping out *bubbemeisers*. All over Boston, New England. Telegrams he sends her, messages. A married woman, my Mirl. I'm crazy? You think *I'm* crazy? Did *I* tell my daughter, shave your *head*? Run around *bald*? Make like a Krishna Hari Kari? Bare feet, a cup, begging? In the worst years, depression, debts, bankrupt, a five-and-dime running on pennies, did I dance in the street for our customers? Show my legs?

"Mirl! Mirl! Hand over the kids. I'll kill. My angels, please, at least put on shoes, socks. Runny noses, look pneumonia already. Home, come on, I'm taking them home. Mirl, listen, mine! They're mine. It's my grandchildren. I can't have my own flesh and blood?

"Crazy? Who looks crazy? This Mirl in the bare feet, in a bedspread, or me, the Grandma, dressed up, a lady? You want I should look like her officer? You'll believe me? Look, no shoes, no stockings, girdle, I'll go around naked … Let go, let go of my girdle! Mirl help, help. Officer, are you crazy? I'm just showing, teaching a lesson. I'm teaching my daughter a lesson. Public! Do *I* want to do it in public? On the Boston Common? Come home, Mirl, come home, I'll show. In private. Children, my children, my *bubbeles, kindelach*, help! Mirl help! I didn't do anything, take it. Take my girdle, dress, panties. I'll sell it in the street to help, help! Ten cents, Max, ten cents! I want to stay, stay! Help!

"I'm not going to stab. I'm calm. Officer, I'm calm. Look, steady, look how steady my hand is. Would I stab my own daughter, officer? It's him. He's the one I want to kill.

"She doesn't want to live with the doctor, all right, don't live with, come home, live with me, Max, the kids, all together like the old days, I'll put ribbons in their hair, hair, make them with my own hands, bibs, booties, cakes, cookies, everyday, kids, see, see, they want to come home, from Grandma they get everything. Mirl, Mirl too, so forget the *farshtoonkenah* doctor. Mamma has room, Mirl, Mamma has room.

"I'm nervous, Officer, that's all. I'm going to keep my girdle on. I'm not going to run around. For her it's all right but not for me. I don't get telegrams. No one stands in front of my door in Brookline and sings from Western Union, 'Shave your head / Stop / Sell your stuff.' See Officer, see, a snake in the grass, you got to be ready, songs, psalms, stab right away, so Western Union can't sing, sing, sing to your wife!

"So I'm crazy. So take me to the crazy house. Shave my head. So I'll be like Mirl. Max, I don't care. I want my babies. I want to be crazy. Make me crazy, doctor, make me like Mirl, no underwear, shoes, nothing, see. I can sing too. 'A *Yiddisha maidel* loves a *Yiddisha mensch*! Ta ta ta tum!' Good, *nu?* Ten cents, I'm sorry. It's a business. I sang. Ten cents!

"Gimme a dime. Gimmmmeeee or I'll … I'm a beggar. I'm begging for the kids. Doctor, you got to give me that dime. No, I won't let go. No—a dime! I'll kill you. A dime! A dime!

"See, I'm good, even from you, I made a dime. In no time I'll make more. See, Mirl, will see.

"No one, all alone, on the Common, the kids, with crazies, let me call, I got a dime, I can call. I'll tell her, come here! The doctor, everyone—crazy! You can dance on the lawn, sing, free meals, even kosher. I'll call. Let me call. I'm calling. Mirl! Mirl! Kindeh! Kindeh?

"They can't hear. Can't hear. I'll kill 'em. I'll kill. Kill.

"Okay, okay, I'm calm. I'm calming down. I can understand. I can't call the Boston Common. I can't call anyone. I can't collect dimes. I can't go home. I can't see the kids. I can't talk to Max. I can't go out. I can't *pish*. I can't open my mouth. I cccca … I cccca …cccc …

"Kill! Kill!

"Calm, no. I'm calm.

"I'm coming. I'm coming with the doctor. Only the doctor didn't do nothing, doctor, didn't do nothing for me the doctor, Mirl says for me the doctor doesn't do nothing: nothing, no more doctor, doctor, do you know the doctor? The doctor who didn't do nothing, nothing?

"Nothing! Don't do nothing. Doctors don't do nothing. I don't want nothing. Nothing. Get away. Nothing! Nothing!

"No, I know. I know, no. No one else is crazy. No, I'm crazy. No, I know. I know, no. No one, just me. I'm crazy.

"See, I'm crazy.

"No, no one, me.

"See, I'm healthy.

"Ha, ha, ha, ha. No, no one. Maxie and me, no, I don't want to see, no, but I owe, here, for Max, a penny.

"No, I'm not going to go. See, I'm crazy. I'm healthy. Peepeepee … peepeepee … peepee …

"Max can the kids make peepee? Can you make peepeepee? Like me. I'm making peepeepeepeepee … It's healthy.

"Oooo, a bad girl, Mirl, a bad girl, the bad girl has to go, has to go, Max, the bad girl has to go.

"I'm going. I understand. I'm going. Somewhere else. It's not so nice. I understand. It's only for awhile, maybe. When I'm not so crazy. Me. See, when I don't make peepee. See.

"Oh o! Oh o! Oh o! I know. I know. Oh o! Oh o!

"So, so, sooo …"

Her arm caught in bronze fingers, Mirl's mother heard the trill of a bird answering her, the selfsame laughing note echoing in the bushes, beds around her, hundreds.

"The cuckoo! Around the house, the form, the case, the knife, cuckoo, cuckoo!

"So, faker, so. You know? You saw? Where? In the air? Ha, ha, ha, ha. Doctor! *Doctor*? Come here! I want everyone to hear. Shhhhhh? Why shhhhhhhh?

"*Doctor*, this is a doctor, listen, you'll see, who is crazy, him or me?

"Shhhh …why? Am I? You don't care, he sees him in the air? So, so, so, so where?"

The lady is explaining to the bronze statue of an Indian gripping her arm that still clasps a knife, her enlightenment a few hours before in Mattapan. Her flailing free hand indicates the doctor who is her doctor, turning away, the doctor who is a patient, smiling up at her from his bed, his finger cautioning her to stay quiet, as she persisted.

"When he comes down from the air? Over there? Right there?

"See I believe it, see. I'm not so crazy. I got to find him quick.

"Sick, who's sick? You're sick, not me," she repeated her question to the prone, still battered man, whom she had recognized. "Look, right on a dime, I can make peepee, me!

"You are still *farcuckt*, Doctor. You understand? On your pants, pajamas, hands. All over, wipe. You got to wash yourself, keep clean, like this, see what I mean. Don't stare, Mister, get him a fresh pair.

"I can't go, why? Look, my pants are dry.

"All the time, right on a dime. I'm well. I can't stand the smell. I got to go. No, I don't want to make a call." She tried to indicate the doctor who *is* her doctor. "It's all over. I got to wait? How many weeks? One, two, what am I going to do? You'll see? Occupational therapy? Look, I want to cook. Okay, I'll do whatever you say. Just move me away. From where? From that bunch that sees things in the air. Oh, you didn't know. Not me, nothing. I didn't see. Never mind, I don't want to talk, nurses, doctors. Think I'm crazy? Just take a walk. Half awake. I'm fine, do my hands shake? *Kreplach*, *taiglach*, *tcholent*, I'll bake. Why? Doctor, I understand. I'm not going to cry, just let me try. You'll see, for you, double butter, lemon special, my momma's best, a cake. A cake!

"So you got to cut the cake. Cut the cake thin, so thin you can't see the cake, just the cutter, because he cut me out, he cut me out of my cake, my cookies, he cut me, but now I'm out, I'm going to cut, cut. I'm going to kill him. I'll kill him. Kill!"

In the mist, copper sinews twisted around the silver handle of the knife. "A killer," moaned Mirl's mother as she struggled in the Indian's arms. Her bosoms shivered as the Ponkapoag and she toppled to the ground. Even as she let go of the cake cutter, she clung still to his wrists and Chickatabot found himself entangled in the softest flesh he had ever felt, rolls of sweet white fat, dough of beaten egg fluff and sugar. The lady wouldn't let go but kept crying, "Killer! Killer!" He couldn't help it. She smelled of bruised purple petals, violets. Her thin silk nightgown slid under him as she pushed and pulled. He snuggled against her breasts, thighs, and took a nip in her neck. He heard groans. Waves of tears washed over him. It was the first time since the Great Depression that anyone in lust had embraced Mirl's mother.

"Oy, you killer."

Tom toms were beating in Chickatabot's ears. She was tugging at the strings of his shirt, leggings. "We'll go naked. No girdle. Nothing."

He tried to roll with the lady toward the lean-to. A cake knife nicked his knee. A curtain of haze, thick and soporific as the scent of pond lilies came down on the red and white beast of two backs. Cuckoos were howling in the bushes.

Dum dum dum dum

Dumb dumb dumb dumb
Dum dum dum dum
Money orders c/o Mattapan

Synagogue Youth

Maishe Ostropol is about to say good-bye. Where? In the sanctuary, his hideout is the last place anyone would look—a boarded-up synagogue on Fowler Street. This is the *shul* of his childhood. A baby, he clambered over and under the benches, sipping orange soda, ginger ale, whiskey, from his grandfather's cup, crumbling sponge cake in his lap.

His wife, Rochelle, unaware of his presence is wandering in dusty pews, a snow leopard stalking her footsteps. Mustapha, whose storefront church closed long ago, is curled up in the last row on a pillow of old prayer shawls. Reilly, his cohort in crime, is still in a coma, locked up behind a tattered, velvet curtain in the ark of the law. The cracks between boards across the windows light engine parts scattered all over the floor, wheels, cables, and chains. A few motorcycles are parked in the aisle. Bearded outlaws, black and white, sleep here and in the study behind the prayer hall.

Caravans of squad cars, six, eight, ten, dissect the streets of Roxbury, Dorchester, Mattapan—squinting with hostile eyes, searching for persons fitting their description in the doorways of Black Boston while the neighborhood stares back angrily. Mustapha, Lennie the Shtoup, the old chiefs of Blue Hill Avenue crime are scared. No one is taking orders. A Black man in zebra skins, calling himself the King of Blue Hill Ave., has come to visit the synagogue and warned Mustapha to get rid of Whites in the building. "Ain't proper," the man warned. "You got to purify yourself."

"I don't understand you, brother," Mustapha protested. "You a Muslim?"

"I am beyond all that," said the King who was eight feet tall. "I am in the land of Og and Baal."

Before Mustapha could open his mouth, hundreds of kids bubbled out of the backyards and alleys around the synagogue, filled the front stairs, windows, doorways, armed with small Saturday night specials, straight razors tucked into belts around yellow baseball jackets.

"You got White people walkin' round equal to Black. It got to stop."

"You got it wrong, brother," said Mustapha.

"Royal highness, Omnipotent, All Bright Radiance to *you*, fatso."

"All Bright, I swear, these Whites are just my slaves."

"Show me."

"Bow down boys," Mustapha intoned, blinking and winking, "Kiss my bronze buttocks."

A sea of Saturday night specials waved as the paler motorcyclists conformed.

"I am going to make a sacrifice of one," crowed Mustapha. He ran back to the ark and pulled the curtain on a comatose Reilly. "Folded up and doped. Waiting for the right moment with the moon. I'm going to cut his heart out, just for you."

The King of Blue Hill Ave. hummed. He and his army stepped back from the synagogue doors, windows, then stopped. He saw the white form of the rabbi's wife, wandering erect among the benches with the spotted cat while the rest of the *shul's* occupants bowed before him. "What's she doing here?"

"An albino black," cried the reverend. "Want to tangle with a herd of elephants? Beware, All Bright."

"Listen you!" The King pulled three hundred trembling pounds up into the air by the nape of the neck. "Don't try to make no calls. I just might feed you to my men." The kids hummed together, smiling, smacking their lips. "You understand Armageddon?"

"Mmmmm," mumbled Mustapha.

"I am Armageddon!" the King declared, dropping the preacher in the aisle. "Coal!" He chanted, "I am coal and combustible gas."

Six hundred Saturday night specials shattered the sky. The Fowler Street Synagogue shivered in a sea of yellow baseball jackets.

Mustapha tried to summon his runners, numbers men, storefront strong-arms, but they were harassed with rocks from rooftops, broken windshields, flaming arrows, pistol shots. The older hoodlums were scared off the side streets, then the avenue. The *Shtoup* wouldn't send in Italians, Portuguese or Puerto Ricans and Mustapha couldn't get out. He stared up now from the pew where he was sleeping, "Fletcher!"

"What's that?"

"Got to talk with you." The two tiptoed out of the prayer chamber into a hallway of the crumbling house of study. Mustapha unlocked the cracked oak door of the upstairs washroom and they stepped into a dusty water closet, its mirror in cobwebs that held in place the shattered glass. Faucets and taps had calcified into green stumps and red rust. The water from an abandoned main, sweated drop by drop through the gnarled root of a broken pipe.

"Ah seen her husband."

"What husband?" asks Fletcher.

"You ever see elephants kneel down and cry? Rubbin' big noses in the dirt? Ah seen him in your cage. Talked to me too," Mustapha whispers with wide open eyes.

"What he say?"

"Goin' to take the elephants into Roxbury. Make me a promise," he begs.

"Depends."

"Just don't laugh."

"Can't promise *that*," Fletcher says.

"I saw Hebrew letters around his head. Kind you read on the walls here. Those gals I used to trade out of the back of the Cadillac were here, pointing their fingers at me, sad."

The reverend puts the keeper's hand on the shrunken folds of his face. They are wet as seal's flesh. "I saw *your* elephants. Painted with that Jewish star. Not one or two chewed up beasts. Dozens—they were coming down Seaver Street. Every time I go to sleep, I hear praying. I see Moses' wife, the Ethiopian, a carving knife in her hand, bloody. Those patriarchs I preached about, shakin' their fingers. I keep bleedin' every time I go to the latrine. Fletcher, ah done you wrong."

"I didn't take it poisanal."

"The day is coming."

"I know."

"Fletcher, get me out of here."

"Can't."

"Please," begs the reverend. "Lights coming on and off nights. Don't know where I am. Windows chattering in their sashes like dry bones is about to rise. I got to go. Lord! Lord!"

"You got to wait," whispers the keeper to the weeping Mustapha.

"Why? Why?"

"You got to uplift this trash alongside you."

"I can't stand the sight of the scum, mixed multitude. Bad company."

"You bring the good word to them."

"Haw. How you think these children going to take it?"

"Try. No harm in that." The keeper swings Mustapha away from the latrine and turns him back toward the prayer hall. "I heard you talking so sweet, no girl can pass you by."

"Can't," coughs the reverend, on his knees among the motorcycle gang sprawled in the pews.

"Pray," urges his friend, squeezing the damp palm in his own.

"There he is. Oh my. There he is!"

"It's him, that boy."

"Maishe," calls the lady. The leopard by her side begins to glow.

There in the motes of the ceiling's inverted bowl hangs the specter of Rabbi Moses Ostropol. His wife floats up towards him into the dim shadows of the cupola.

Rachel and Moses: two halves of the same story, holy sister and brother who never meet. "Kiss me," the congregation hears the voice forcing itself out of the corners of the synagogue so that the wall shudders. "Kiss me."

Her lips graze flesh, leather, and a clap of fire hurtles from the ceiling, singeing the leopard's coat, electrifying Mustapha and Fletcher's hair, crashing in a bolt into the ark which bursts into flames.

"Reilly," they shout. The two run up on the bema, pull the burning velvet curtains away, and fling the carved walnut cabinet open. The inside of the ark is charred.

"Is he alive?"

"No sign." But just then, a patch of red burnt flesh upon his forehead, the naked man springs erect and bursts toward the synagogue doors, flinging them open, running out into the street, where all is pandemonium.

The Rabbis' Shpitz

"**C**... C ... Can he h ... h ... hear us?"

Of course he can. Every pebble in the puddingstone under his ear rings clear as a timpani. He can even answer. Only he is a little backward, abashed. In time, if you are right about instructing him, he will be compelled to enter the argument.

"C ... C ... Can we p ... p ... proceed?"

Am I stopping? I'm the bad guy? Already? You get that tooth in at the right moment—a soft answer, stick me with the nasty reply. Am I against proselytes? Just because I didn't indulge in a stable of them, I'm anti-the-nations?

"T ... T ... Touchy."

Who gets himself inscribed a friend of the poor, proletarian? Ishmael is the creep, fat cat. You got the touch. You finagled every letter of the Torah. According to you a man is judged by the deeds of his father. So, you know this bum's *zaidee*? By me, I'm only asking, did Seamus here do good or evil? Is he well plastered? Can he hold a drop?

"L … L … Let him s … s … speak."

So speak, speak. Am I sitting in his mouth obstructing entrance, egress? Let the flood of Cheba come out of his jaws.

"Wherein …" began the Gael timorously.

"W … W … Wonderful. A wonderful s … s … start."

Shaaaah.

"Wherein," began the Gael again, buoyed on the tide of Ishmael's concern, "does the gift of Hebrew scripture differ from the sweet melody of the Tain Bo Culaigne?"

Dummy! Blockhead! Booby. That bunch of *bubbemeisers* to be compared with the testament of Moses?

"P … p … please."

Say, shrieked the skull of Ishmael, everything in that cattle breeder's chronicle, bull hide of baloney were 100 percent true, no holds barred, what really happened. What's it to you?

"What's it to?" the Irish officer repeated, stumbling over the unfamiliar song.

"Wh … Wh … Who's your f … favorite?"

"Favorite?"

"Wh … Wh … Who? I … I … In the b … b … book."

"'Tis the swift slashing, flesh ravenous, raven fierce fighter, the fiery, furious, ferocious lion against whom you would find few to match for youth, vigor, strength, sternness, stalking, scheming or slaughter, the sweet-breathed, clear-eyed, Cuchulain."

"*N … N … Nu?*"

"*Nuuuu*," whinnied the son of Inishowen fashioning his lips and nose to the strange incantation.

"W … W … What's it t … t … to you?"

"What's it to?" echoed the policeman.

Do you profit, *nu*? Dunderhead, dimwit, what do *you* get? I got to stick your nostrils in the dust. Smell, Golem! Sniff, breathe, suck, what?

"W …W … What?"

Nothing! shouted Ishmael.

The earth on which the body of Seamus lay—shook. The seismographic machine doctors had craftily hooked up among the hundreds of wires, tubes, loops, running off the prostrate policeman in the hospital bed, registered a cataclysm. They rushed in from the corridor to regard the blank face of the officer, marvel at the humming, buzzing along the wires. Sounds of intolerable sweetness filled that floor of the Boston City Hospital, faint in the ears of its nurses, patients, doctors, but unbalancing.

"N … N … Noodle. U … U … Use your k … k … *kopp*."

"Nothing?" repeated Seamus before the sages.

Nothing for nothing? You got to get something.

"T …T …Tricky b … b … business."

Kuni Lemel. You got to look out for yourself. First, forget those fairy tales. A handful of images, idols. First is *you*! Get a foot out of the grave. If you are going to believe, the first rule—fix a place up for yourself.

"A foot?"

"A f … f … foot!"

A foot, a toe, even a pimple will do, as long as it's you, Ishmael added.

The officer shook his head, confused.

"R … R … Res-eee … rection."

"I've heard of that," whistled Seamus.

Of course you have. Nothing new. Only with us, it's tit for tat. You give us this, we'll give you that.

"Only there are religions too, who …"

"D … D … Don't start Seamus."

We stick with a simple deal. Us for *You*, *You* for us.

"Us?" Seamus asked Rabbi Ishmael.

"Ha, ha, ha," the two rabbis laughed together.

"W … W … We got a g … g … good deal."

A little further back, Shammy, one of us worked out a contract, second to none, just two clauses. All along, Noah to Abraham, we were working on it. But we got the language straight a hundred, two hundred years before Akiba. In short, "If I'm not for myself," as Hillel says, "who will be for me?"

"R …R …Right away it c … c … covers you!"

"But," quoted Ishmael, "if I am only for myself, who am I?"

"C … C … Covers everyone."

Group coverage, everyone or no one.

"N … N … Not exclusive."

No, we included the whole *mishpochah*, pagans, Arabs, Jews, third world. Some day we figured, we'll expand operations. Why box oneself in? What do we get for it? Rabbi Ishmael asked, his voice rising. A kick in the *tzittsies*. It starts with everyone against us. It ends, we're afraid to be for ourselves.

"So," wavered the voice of the officer. Tooth and skull scraped the earth, hearing a familiar melody. "How come you are here?"

A hoarse rattling disturbed the turf. "P ... P ... Pretty g ... g ... good."

We're waiting, said Ishmael.

"Waiting?"

We could take a meal ticket now, put on a robe. I hear from some, we got a full dress one waiting. Snappy outfit, inwrought gold, tailor-made, every pious act, Ishmael, Akiba, did, sparkling, only who wants to hang around, singing, waiting?

"Waiting?" the officer asked Rabbi Ishmael.

We're waiting, the big day, everyone else gets up, a new deal, Messiah.

"The Messiah?" queried Seamus.

"*Meshiach ben Dovid*," the rabbis sang. In the hospital room, the staff watched the seismograph register plates rising under the sea, continents moving against each other: Africa and America nuzzling; Asia slowly turning round to embrace the couple as a third; a gradual incomprehensible roll, the earth wobbling on its axis.

The skull of Ishmael boiled gold out of its cracks. The tooth of Akiba seethed in a steam of pearls, thickened to a column of ivory. The Gael smelled the fifteen odors of paradise, which ascending, cling to the heavenly garments of the patriarchs. His eyes watered with the precious rheum of bdellium, the dew of the Holy One, blessed be He.

"How about a resurrection now?"

"N ... N ... Now?"

"Just to show it isn't all blarney," the officer whispered.

"Y ... Y ... You want to go b ... b ... back?"

"Just to give the folks a start. Sort of demonstrate— what it's all about."

"W ... W ... Well. I ... I ... Ishy?"

Listen Shammy. It's not with us to do such things. To huck in your ear is no trouble. To pick and wind you up again—another thing. We're rabbis, not prophets. Teaching, all right. Miracles ceased with Ezra. We're happy right here, waiting for Messiah. You got another religion in mind, raising the dead. Talk to them. We're not getting up until the Day of Judgment. My bones are tired. Once is enough in this world. I'm waiting for the next one.

"But I'm not dead."

"R ... R ... Right."

"Technically, there's no doctor's certificate out on me."

"T ... T ... True."

"If I get up and move around for awhile I wouldn't be violating any dogma."

"F ... F ... For a *sh ... sh ... shpitz*, Itzy?"

A joke? said Rabbi Ishmael. I'm always ready for a joke, Akiba. Maybe as a joke we could get away with it.

The two shards, bone and tooth, bent toward each other in the loose soil. A trickle of moisture oozed from a split in a lump of stone under the officer. In the hospital room nurses began to swoon. "Oh God, God!" Fine wires, tubing, blood vessels, were snapping, breaking, bursting on all sides.

Hospital Patience

Ready for a miracle, barefoot, the doctor rises and walks out on the uncombed lawn through a miasma of paradise, daffodils, violets—his upper lip wet. A ribbon of green dots wheels in the air currents over the Hub. Particles of centuries-old gas that had settled in the Neponset marshes, congealed on the rubbery bark of kelp, blown away into the atmosphere, are rising and falling again. A column of emerald mist, invisible to the eye, streams down from the stratosphere to the Fort Point Channel. Its haze is drifting toward Roxbury.

In his head, the doctor sees an army of elephants, the war tanks of the Carthaginians, Syrian and Hasmonean kings. The shapes of the clouds begin to assume body, substance. The doctor laughs as the patients appear at the windows, doors, the psychiatrists, nurses, among them, wide eyed, gaping. Madness can be smelled, tasted in the city. Boston is about to …

Boston Rejoice!

Godi, Fiorenza, poi che sé sì grande
che per mare e per terra batti l'ali
e per lo 'nferno tuo nome si spande!

Joy, Florence, since you are so grand,
that over sea and land you beat your wings
and through Hell itself, your name expands!
  Dante Alighieri, *La Divina Commedia*

From cellar holes as the poisoned wind dissipated, S. J. and his minions rose. His followers had been in the thick of the inferno. It was weeks before the sun bleached the green from their raw pink cheeks. Yet the commissioner *was* out of the way, his squad of sergeants blown sky high.

A ghastly luminescence lit the faces of all close to the cone. They stared at their neighbors garbling words, mingling slogans with obscenity, stirring in the certainty of what it was about. The corridors and offices of city hall were crowded with thousands of petitioners: housewives, street corner alcoholics, young thugs, moving ceaseless with some mumble that the mayor could only catch snatches of, but which he knew he had to memorize before the next election. He and the rest of the vast clerical staff bent their ears to mimic until they were mouthing the jam, saying something, but what? The press was struggling with the new stuff but to the rest of the country looking in, it seemed as if Boston was witless. Mayor O'Blank appeared on the bulging blue tube shouting at a mob in one of the white neighborhoods, "It *was* a great city, right?" There were cheers. Black fingers too were grasping at the mayor's coat, his secretaries' skirts. He preferred to smile rather than talk to the minority voting groups. But he did promise, and made it sound like a campaign pledge, "Something awful's going to happen."

Little drops of green congealed on the ground. A sweet odor at the edge of fence boards, on the stumps of trees, while trash rotted in backyards at a tropical rate. Spots of fungus broke out on the brick fronts of Charlestown. They burst and the red clay began to crumble. Homeowners scrubbed with acid, swabbed with shellac. Washington, DC, was drawn into the neighborhood when a patch of mold began to climb up the Bunker Hill Monument, pimpling the stone. The inspectors scratched their heads over it, ears, necks and backs. The physicians had no answers. In the panic that seized the federal office building when spots appeared on its desks and tables—all government agencies cooperated—a specialist from the Department of Agriculture diagnosed—cattle murrain. Under the stethoscope it appeared as a rogue virus: its symptoms similar to a plague never seen by modern science, a faint serpentine ribbon of yellow weeping mucous out of open sores, leaping by proximity. It resembled a scab of the seventeenth century, the delusion of Irish farmers in the face of a virulent hoof-and-mouth, the County Kerry botch.

While this infestation only made the inhabitants of Bunker Hill, Bartlett, and Sullivan Street testier in their clothes, fumigated in part by alcohol: *Three Roses* and *Thunderbird*, the U.S. marshals who had swarmed up in starched shirts to protect the monument were defenseless. They fought off the urge to reach into powdered underwear; instead struck out at passersby, in particular teenage hoods of the street corners who whistled when they rubbed the lampposts. Fever and chills in the morning, a rise in irritability through the afternoon, hallucinations at the hour of dusk, scratchiness through the night; it spread through Boston, fastening with virulence on its police. The botch burrowed in wool shakers, prickled until it provoked a man to thump. Under the former commissioner, the constabulary sat to the side while the factions in the city tickled each other. Now the blue coats butted in, whacking at will. The general fever rose highest around the monument where the citizens dared the cops to protect outsiders. The locals didn't want Blacks, Hispanics, Jews, Harvard professors, or any upward bound middle class, native to Charleston or not —hanging around. It began with pushing and shouting. The police rattling batons, the neighborhood began to go after the men in blue in lieu of the minorities who had skedaddled. The battles escalated. Down the steep sides of Breed's Hill, where the British had turned tail twice before the ragged backsides of Charleston's colonials, the tactical police thundered in formal riot gear, firing shotguns into the air, lead-tipped nightsticks wagging at their hips, but outmaneuvered by a knot of mothers gathered with broken beer bottles, infants in their arms, to pray against the cops. Women pushed the officers back upon the sharp, flat spears of the Monument Square fence, screaming, "Mother muggers!"

Well-wishes poured from every window ledge. The police, who had charged into the tear gas they exploded before them, confused by a hail of sticks and stones, flailed to the left, unable to keep the ranks of their phalanx intact in the open space of Monument Square. Caught in a narrow web of cross lanes behind the high school, Jefferson, Green, Cross, Trenton, Cord—garbage bags full of gasoline, a trash barrel stuffed with nails and cherry bombs, planks ripped off the surrounding fences—peppered the officers. With flaming trousers, the tactical police, T.P.F., wheeled, coats smoking, while sirens wailed through Boston, "National Guard."

"National Guard! National Guard!" pleaded the new commissioner. The head of the T.P.F. had lost his eggs in Cedar Street. The toughs treaded him insensible on top of broken baby bottles and left him hanging on the iron fence upright by the monument. Leaderless, the police were barricaded in the monument and the high school. "National Guard! National Guard!" The phones were going off like a fire alarm system in His Honor's office. O'Blank was lodged securely in a false-bottomed drawer of his desk, a safety compartment he had designed. There were two weeks of dried cod, pickled beets, and Jack Daniels in an adjoining drawer. "No," he whispered into the mouthpiece of the receiver beside him. Charlestown—where voting machines rolled out of the graveyards to tally up pluralities? His aides were frantic, the governor, the president, half the country was on the line trying to get him to ask for the Guard but O'Blank was not about to be the one responsible. "Never!" When the flag broke out on top of the Bunker Hill shaft and a policeman hung by his heels below it for a few moments, the governor, watching from the top of the statehouse's gold dome with binoculars, pulled out the last wisp of his light brown hair and admitted defeat, "Order them in."

The troop transports standing by at the Boston Army Base shoved off, the Yankee Doodle Division. They fingered automatic rifles, with twenty-five pound flak jackets, packs full of pots, pans, shovels. Bows scraped the pilings of the Hoosac Pier as they filed from the boats by Old Ironsides. Word spread down Warner, Main, Medford Street to City Square, Thompson, Sullivan Square. Not even the squad of T.P.F. who had barricaded themselves on the top floor of the high school could believe it.

The fastest retreating division in the American Army—its secret, a leg jerk, the "Yankee step," famed from Bull Run to Bastogne, as the one always held in reserve, its battle cry, "Another Day." Going into action? Bombs immediately blew up the last spans of the Charleston and Warren Avenue bridges as a telescope buried in the weeds of Boswell Lane peered at the sweat pouring off the faces of the division's officers, landing.

Ordinarily the Yankees liked nothing better than to strut an afternoon on hazardous duty pay after the police had done the dirty work. From across the waves, off the sides of the State Street Trust and the Custom House tower the shouts from Charlestown had rung. Shortwave radios had informed them of the rest. The commanding general asked for a few barrages from the battleships in mothballs off the army base. "Just to clear the streets." But the governor balked. "Guadalcanal? Iwo Jima? You lay down a firestorm, level the ground," explained the general.

"And where was the air force?" he asked. The governor shouted terrible things at him. The general had to remind His Excellency of a brother, head of the State Liquor Authority, a brother-in-law, attorney general. But when the governor went on with his demand that the Guard get right up to the monument, the general snarled, "Since you're so bloodthirsty, come in yourself with a few state police.

"The first rule," he resumed, restraining his temper, "of an amphibious landing is to secure a safe bridgehead. Accumulate sufficient store to ensure superiority: trucks, tanks, atomic cannon ..." Several sergeants had already had stones thrown at them slipping into the doorway of a saloon in the no-man's-land of City Square. At present half his staff wanted to rocket the streets, while others warned they would resign commissions if anyone pulled a trigger.

In the middle of explaining his tactic—*make a demonstration at the edge of Charlestown while evacuating the T.P.F. off the top of the high school by helicopter*—the general dropped the phone. A moment before, from the bay waters in the late afternoon, a mist had risen—gray flannel with spots of green. It wintered the brass of Old Ironsides and shook the sockets of the general. His men, a majority from outlying suburbs, had never felt the tingle of the harbor algae.

It seeped in droplets through the weft of their green cotton fatigues, congealed in the sweaty bunching of woolen socks. The troops shivered, shook. Rubbing gun barrels, bayonets, the division scratched, squirmed. "Form up!" shouted the sergeants. "Parade Rest."

"Bayonets on the ready."

The division moved. Not down Chelsea Street at the edge of town as the general had assured the Charlestown mothers, well in advance, but to its interior, the green space of the training field. Not slowly, cautiously, as agreed upon, but in an open jeep, speeding ahead of his men now in the pea-green fog its commander came on, his staff stumbling after, shouting; following the Bunker Hill Day Parade route backward because, like the British, his troops had to come into the hostile peninsula from Boston. The ladies and their auxiliaries had stationed school children with plastic bags of inflammable rubbish and gasoline in Pepsi-Cola bottles above the abandoned police station in City Square. The march to the right up Winthrop Street threw them off guard and Yankees poured into Monument Square liberating the T.P.F. On the golden dome in Boston, the governor (through binoculars) beside the general, observed the beefy T.P.F. sergeant come down from the top of Breed's Hill and what looked like a local mother go up in the folds of a banner "Never."

"Strike a medal," he called, dancing on one foot.

"Oh no. No!" The aides and secretaries were screaming. His Excellency was sliding down the slippery dome like a greased pig.

Nor could the troops sweeping over the top of Breed's stop to secure the hill. The commanding officer had a moment of lucidity. He struggled with the seat of his pants, and shouted, "Stop!" But the division came on behind, driven by the prick and tumbled over the side of Breed's into the weir of the tiny side streets strung with piano wire where the infants from City Square had been redeployed.

Charlestown! Toothless crones rose from their sick beds. The drunks hanging on the cyclone fence of the housing project came to their senses. Toddlers stepped out of their baby strollers, waddled to the door. Book-ends, bureaus, old boilers, two-by-fours, Lally columns, discharged upon the heads of the Yankees, from the upper windows, lengths of sewer pipe. The soldiers appeared at the ends of alleys, running a gauntlet in which they were stripped of patches, pistols, pants, socks, some of them scalped. Only the quick step saved them. They leapt from their captors' hands, through the showers of nails, bricks, pumping down the side of Breed's, up the top of Bunker. Despite his bulk, the general was out in front. The division would have piled out of Charlestown through Sullivan Square but a pillar of sweetness rose up from Schrafft's. The candy factory was on fire. A cloud of chocolate swept through the street and globs of boiling caramel lapped the rotary. "To the right!" cried the general. "Right! Right!" Then, a word, never heard before by the Yankees, since their first muster in American history.

His Excellency had the satisfaction of seeing it, just before, striking the Bullfinch pediment he shot through his window into the skies of Boston—the thrilling effect of the command. The division wheeled, went right back through the jaws of Charlestown but this time down the main thoroughfare, Bunker Hill Street, to their commander's shout. On all sides, the soldiers called it, outstripping him, through the rabble from the housing projects, through the gates of the U.S. Navy Yard, over the piers, into the waves of the harbor and the waters of the Mystic, which put an end to the tickle, "Forward!"

• • •

The mayor climbed out of his drawer to congratulate the Guard on the dispatch with which it had calmed Charlestown. "In and out! A neat business!" Telegrams of congratulation were crackling into Boston from all over the country. "Forward." The governor in bed with a broken neck was not receiving calls. He had come down like a pigeon shell on the Beacon Hill brick. Charlestown mollified—it could keep any government surplus in its hands.

Boston was quiet. The police had had enough. The governor was in no condition to stick his nose in. The country was told a tale of military aggression which none of the locals was anxious to contradict.

• • •

Word of the troubles had brought fame to the city. Flam MacFardel, whose column, syndicated as it proclaimed, "wherever hard noses stirred to the sound of the harp," arrived. He headed for the downtown bars, following a route of sawdust and urine, found his quarry on the floor of a Charlestown social club. Flam's head matted in holy dust where John Boyle O'Reilly's dog had lingered, "Do, do, do you tink?" he warbled to the veteran beside him. Dawson's ale drained out of both their ears. "Tah boys here really dislike the Black folks?"

His mate yawned, snored, bubbles of rotgut popped through his tooth holes.

Boston Dispatch

FLIM FLAM

```
I was in Charlestown last
night social-lizing with some
of the genuine Celts.
None of your lickspittle sub-
urban lace curtain ladies with
English regimentals around
their white collars, but the
spud shaking article that
keeps the clear, sweet
sound of Galway burbling in
the throat.
There was Tom McGinty, a fine
```

spring rain of a man. "Tom," I
asked. "No nonsense, what are
your thoughts on the problem
of Blacks and Whites?"
"Flam," he answered, putting
a soft, fatherly hand on my
shoulder, letting me feel the
weight of seventy years scraping a living off the docks of
a cold morning on the Charlestown waterfront. "I'm totally
indifferent."

• • •

From the horse's mouth, the
real people, the poor people, the salt of the earth,
fine spring rain, soaked down
Charlestown Irish are unbiased
and don't give a tinker's damn
for nonsense or racial violence in Boston.

• • •

Flam leaned back against the streetlight supporting
him at the corner of A and West Broadway, penning his
column in a loose-leaf notebook at six in the morning.
Someone had dropped him in South Boston, but an
unfamiliar hand yanked at his coat sleeve. The tweed
arm of his jacket came away in a man's fist.

"What are you up to?

"Why you f …" Flam prepared to swing. Seven beet
red faces stared at him, broken Budweiser tops in hand.
"Writing," he continued, adjusting his face to an affa-
ble grin.

"You wouldn't be a reporter, would you?" Flam caught the menace in the question, and the story of a *Globe* correspondent tarred and feathered here, flashed through his thoughts.

Squinting into the glint of blue and green eyes, struck off the sharp edges of the brown glass bottles, their jagged edges, he declaimed, "A freelance singer of tah old songs."

"Where are yuh from?" growled the reddest face.

Flam smiled. "Brooklyn."

"There's a lot of fairies there," one of the men said in an undertone. "What are you doin' heah?" asked another.

"I come up to lend my support," said the reporter, graciously.

"Who asked yuh?" the beet-cheeked leader snatched his notebook. "We bettah show it to S. J."

"S. J.?" asked MacFardel. He had heard of the priest. "I'd like to meet him."

"Sure!" Seven voices assented and as many beer bottles cracked on Flam's skull. The reporter awoke in a basement smelling of embalming fluid, temples banging with pain. A fiery-nosed man with a shock of white hair was staring into Flam's face. "The Resurrection and the Life," rang the voice as soon as the reporter opened his eyes.

S. J. had uncorked a bottle of Pot Still under their two bright noses and the scent of it mingled with the fumes of mortuary alcohol and incense. Every breath through Flam's nostrils seared his head. The Jesuit priest appeared behind a veil of smoky peat, his face a burning apparition. As the bottle emptied, the reporter sank back. He woke again, to find himself propped on the lamppost in the South Boston streets. It was night. His notebook was stuck in his pocket. Flam's tweed jacket sleeve was stitched crudely back to its armhole.

• • •

The local papers had opened their columns to another syndicated analyst, Custiss Attactus, a former minister, Georgia state senator, one time Democratic national committeeman. Custiss arrived the day after Flam.

Boston Dispatch

TRUST US IN CUSTISS

I took a drive down Blue Hill Ave. to old family friends in that garden spot, Grove Hall, Roxbury. As Blacks have moved into this area, the unseemly commercial bustle that sullied this *now* gracious avenue in the days of its former denizens has disappeared. Most of the parasitic merchants packed their baggage and fled in the face of residential disapproval. One can stroll under the shade of century old trees along Blue Hill Avenue hearing the pleasant accents of Savannah, Charleston—(Not Charles*town*, baby!). I sat down to a repast of

creamy hominy grits and but-
tered turnip greens on Creston
Street. "Now tell me, is there
any hardness in your hearts,"
I asked, "toward your pale
fellow citizens here in Boston?" And the man of the
family answered: "Eye for
eye, brother. Tooth for
tooth." There it is, brothers,
the Mosaic Code. The Black Man
in Boston is only asking
for elementary scriptural
rights. Jealousy, is what's
behind all this trouble. Who
threw the first stone in the
Boston Massacre? Caused the
American Revolution?
A Black man!
Shot the British officer commanding on Breed's Hill?
A Black Man!
Boston belongs to Blacks! My
man on Creston, Mr. Powhattan,
banged his table.
"We outproduce them." He
pointed to his
sixteen kids. "We beat them at
their own game!" Jobs, houses,
opportunities, *Get it*
up! Or number your
days—Whitey!

• • •

Custiss had exited smiling from the Jones's kitchen,
to find the tires missing from his raspberry Lincoln

Continental and the car sinking into the warm tar of Creston Street. Beads of cologne stood out on his forehead. At the end of the block he could see the whitewalls rolling. "Calm down, chile," urged Powhattan Jones coming out on his porch.

"Call the police!" cried Custiss.

"Ain't no cop goin' to come to Blue Hill Ave. You got to go see the King."

"The King?" Custiss' ears pricked up.

"King of Blue Hill Ave."

"Where?"

"Follow the bouncin' tires," Powhattan wagged his head.

Custiss reached the avenue just as the gang of juveniles wound off it down a side street. Leaping wooden pickets as they rolled down side alleys, into backyards, heaved themselves over the boards of fences, he shouted after them, waving his wallet, "I'll pay."

Arching over a high palisade of cedar posts, strung with barbed wire and a cement wall set with spikes, Custiss came down in a soft carpet of yellow hay and kept sinking, down and down. This is an elephant trap, he thought. A deep drum thudded in his skull, "Bom, bom, bom."

Dust trickled out of his nostrils. "Bom, bom, bom, bom. Bom bee bom." His head throbbed, painfully, the sound inside, then out. "Bom bee bom bom, bom bee bom." A voice intoned deeper than the base of the drum. "Visible and invisible." Bom bee bom. "I am the King." A fume of poppies filled the cavity. It was as strong as a two-ton load of smack jammed up a junkie's veins. Attactus fainted away in the perfume.

> A sweet little lass in a bright yellow jumper is skipping rope, scuffing her black patent leather Mary Janes on the pavement, lifting her winsome face full of freckles in a smile to me, freckles on her upturned nose, freckles on her arms, freckles on her cheeks, freckles on her fingertips, freckles on her knees, freckles all over until all I can see is a great ball of freckles skipping and hopping in front of me and I have to hold on to a lamppost. *That's Southie for you*. A six-year-old skipping rope. The safest neighborhood in Boston.

> "Life," that's what the Reverend S. J. O'Halloran who heads the South Boston Civic Association told me people want. Just a chance to open their mouths wide and taste the briny blue water that sparkles at the foot of the hills where rows of neat, well-kept cottages and wooden three deckers testify to the industry and cohesion of the local in- habitants. Who wants to break up these happy homes?

Our Black neighbors who
are fighting to hold onto
fire traps in apartments in
Roxbury?

   Don't you believe it. The
violence in Boston is a scheme
of the Yankee banks. It's down
in the vaults of the First
National turning their stock
certificates that the finan-
ciers have set their eyes upon
Southern Boston, determined to
drive the householders out
under the pretext of integrat-
ing the neighborhood. They
have their Judas in the may-
or's office, in the police
force, in the courts, so that
the Reverend O'Halloran had to
go into hiding to escape ha-
rassment. It's a Law sold for
three pieces of silver—the
same their fathers and grand-
fathers felt under the lash of
English landlords in Donegal,
Clare, Cork, and Galway.
Their spokesman is not afraid
to speak in the language of
religious faith. Hard pressed,
the Celts of South Boston,
Charlestown, Mission Hill, believe in miracles, the dear
old days of stickball
and James Michael Curley at
the kitchen door. John F. Ken-
nedy romancing the ladies
for a vote, Gaelic football,

```
nickel cigars, Honey Fitz,
diphtheria, "Ah me, I fondly
dream." For the big lie hangs
over Boston, it stinks like
the brach by the fire.
The old story—"they're all
agin' us!"
```

• • •

Custiss looked out the window. The silver sidewalls were back on, someone had given him a free waxing, and the tank was full.

• • •

```
Folks you hear a lot of loose
talk about what a troubled
place Roxbury must be, but I
never, well hardly ever,
spent such a calm, relaxed,
totally at ease, soporific
night and day as I did
with my friend, the King,
lounging at his bad off Blue
Hill Ave. May seem strange to
some of you to call a man "the
King," but that's just what
this big fellow is. He has
done the impossible, scared
the You Know What out of
all those little jive-fingered
junkies, pick-pockets, pimps
and con men who have been the
plague to Black A-merica. This
Man means business, and ORDER.
He's got all those kids off
the street and into step. Blue
```

```
Hill Ave. is high-cotton,
walkin' with the King. Watch
out! He's got the visible, and
the in-visible power. He's
got Hoodoo, the Mojo tooth,
the jaw of Balaam and all
that baaad black Magic wor-
kin'. Yeahh Boston. I heah it
comin'. Black, Black, Black.
Baaam bee laam! Be-ware! This
boy is goin' to give you a
taste of sepa-rate. He's goin'
to separate Boston. Old Sepa-
rate but Equal is about
to take revenge. Separate.
Better separate yourself
from half your goodies. Fast
Be-ware.
```

• • •

"Baam! Doom!" Flam and Attactus collided in the corridor of the local paper. "It's all over!"

"Better believe it!" They pounded each other's tummies and backs, in the elevator down to the bar, drove south to New York City reeking and roaring.

• • •

As the Continental wound up the expressway ramp, a file of young men in green Tam O'Shanters sank into the waters of Fort Point Channel with rubber bags. Under the tar of the highway in a culvert, a row of black youngsters threaded wire cable. A hush settled over Boston.

Attendance even climbed at the local parishes and the cardinal whose joints were twisted in gout as by a grand inquisitor allowed himself a breath. Were people coming to their senses? Or was it a last farewell? The wine was murky in his communion cup. On B street, a lady had given birth to twins of indeterminate sex. The bricks of city hall poured sweat. Lightning twice struck the cathedral and the Mystic River rose to an unusual level. The statue of General Hooker in front of the statehouse was reported to have moved its jaws, horse and rider. The equestrian bronze dripped from its testicles and the ground of the Boston Common subsided in two huge caverns to the subway system.

Colonel O'Cann had been superseded.

Out of Suffolk Jail S. J sprung little O'Coogan, mastermind of the Great Armored Car Robbery. O'Coogan financed successful candidates for city council in the succeeding year but couldn't curb a disposition to shoot at policemen. For unpaid parking tickets, he was lured to a court appearance; clapped in jail, where one thing led to another and he had spent seven years.

The door of his cell swung open.

"Parole?" he inquired.

"A furlough," the sheriff replied, "Better be discreet."

Up and over the wall, O'Coogan fell into the backseat of a convertible where S. J. explained the situation. O'Coogan's eyes lit up. The piping in his brain had been smacked about. Black and White were mere shadows. Hell would dispel the gloom.

Sappers began operating in the streets. There were daily battles. Residents, regardless of their color or religious preference, were at the mercy of firing caps, cans of gasoline ablaze. Gangs swarmed in and out of the touchstones of conflict; Uphams and Fields Corner, Edward Everett and Codman Square. Slowly a line of defense began to form on both sides. Neither party dared to step over the line and between it lay no-man's-land. Not a whisper of what was going on was printed in the papers.

Under O'Coogan's eye, S. J.'s staff abandoned the idea of defensive strategy. Plans were laid for a lightning strike. Commandeering the trucks of the firemen and garbagemen, the Irish would launch a three-pronged panzer attack into Roxbury, pushing most of the Blacks in Mattapan, Dorchester out towards Boston Bay, "The whole kit and caboodle—bagged." Everyone applauded. "Drowned like kitties."

"Couldn't we put them in boats and ship them back to Africa?" asked a former nun. They stuffed a rag in her mouth and shut her up in a wardrobe.

"I tole you guys not let any girls in," piped O'Toole. Skinny had clambered up the ladder of command in O'Cann's place and was now in charge of O'Coogan's praetorians, a picked crew of cutpurses, grave robbers and child murderers.

"How about all the Irish between Dorchester Avenue and the sea?" asked S. J. "Won't they get caught?"

"Lose a few, gain a lot."

"But they're immortal souls … "

O'Coogan grabbed the priest's collar. "Soul?" He pulled S. J. up under his nose. "Seein' things again?" He sniffed. "Better lay off the bottle."

S. J. stormed out of the room. He called O'Cann at his insurance office to arrange a coup d'état. "I'm sorry," he whispered to the colonel. "He's out of control."

• • •

Bleeding profusely, O'Cann sat at his desk, his throat cut, short of breath. When S. J. hurried over to the colonel's office, O'Coogan stepped out of the closet. "Can I help?" he asked the priest.

"What?"

"Couldn't take the pressure." O'Coogan winked, walking past, closing the door behind him on S. J. and the collapsed O'Cann. "Give him a good send off."

• • •

"No sniffling," barked O'Toole back at the conference table. "Your work is cut out for you." Only the nun had slipped out of the wardrobe before they could strangle her. O'Coogan glared at S. J. The priest sucked his thumb. Two praetorians shadowed him everywhere. "No more monkey business."

"She didn't know the details," S. J. intoned. The others assented, grumbling, and sat down to the plan. Quincy, South Boston, the flanks of the Blacks' streets to the north and south were strong. But to herd the Africans into the ocean, the Celts had to get behind them. They would forget the South End, which was full of polite old Negroes from another era and a few white liberals. They could be mopped up later. Columbus Avenue was the strategic artery. Driving down Southampton to Massachusetts Avenue, they would reach the corner of Tremont and proceed as far as Dudley Street where, with reinforcements from Mission Hill, they could strike into the heart of Roxbury, Warren and Blue Hill Ave., stampeding the population. Linking up with a force that would march across Neponset from concealment at the Wollaston Golf Club, the Irish would come up Gallivan Boulevard, half of the phalanx speeding through Codman Square down Talbot Avenue to Blue Hill Avenue where the juncture with the first arrow would occur—in front of Franklin Park. The rest of the second column served as a blocking force to keep Ashmont Street in Irish hands. If the pressure was too great, the Irish could retreat on a second line at Gallivan then hop back over the wide Neponset. It didn't matter if the Blacks drowned in saltwater or fresh. Hyde Park, not as militant, would supply a third pincer to neutralize Mattapan, starting a vigorous fire all along Cummings Highway and ferrying reinforcements along Harvard Street through the cemeteries by the fence of the Mattapan State Insane Asylum to the Talbot Ave. spearhead. Finally—but O'Coogan broke off. "The finishing touch is top secret."

Fleeing a flying squad of O'Coogan's in cabs, combing the approaches to Roxbury for her, the nun fell in with a column of cars heading for asylum at the hospital in Mattapan where large numbers, Black and White, were committing themselves. It was to the doctor that she told her tale.

But it was impossible to keep O'Coogan's presence in South Boston secret. The King's tacticians had proposed a textbook campaign so as to command the natural defenses of the Black streets by sea and land. The threat of O'Coogan called for bolder strategy—a three-foot delinquent joined them, T2, who had left a trail of slashed throats and burning flesh in the juvenile homes of Massachusetts, a child who had been beaten, stamped on so many times he had stopped growing: rattanned, whipped, flailed, until his skin suppurated as raw patch. Under lock and key in maximum security at Walpole, T2 was bustled out to the King in a burlap bag, tumbled through the heating ducts of the prison. He arrived howling in Roxbury but was submerged in a tub of antibiotic ointment. "Under no circumstance," he dictated, "charge the high places. Telegraph, Savin, Mission Hill? No." Crossing the harbor or Neponset was out of the question. Outnumbered it was best to tie the Irish down at the trouble spots, Everett, Codman, Mattapan Square, while making a dash out of Roxbury along Washington Street into downtown Boston and the banks. With the vaults in Black hands, the African Americans could buy the Irish out of town and purchase prime property rather than the cheap stuff they were getting on Dorchester Avenue, the hills, that secondhand housing.

"What happens if they get in here, while we doin' this?" queried the King.

"Good," said T2.

"We goin' to lose a lot of people."

"Better."

"But …" Several of the twelve-year-olds poked the King in the ribs with their pistols.

A green glow played over the tall man's features, its source was the tub. "You just a civilian now, brother," squeaked one of the generals.

"I am the King."

"Them days is over, brother. You got yoah i-de-ol-ogy backward. This here's the Revolution."

"I am …"

"You *old*. We passed the state when you was nec-essary. Put yourself at the service of the Revolution or we goin' to put you to an ad-mini-strated soul-lution."

The tub began to roll toward the door on coaster to the roar of "War!"

• • •

"The nuthouse is nuts," whispered Mirl's mother, waking up in red arms, starting to tell her history. An hour into the monologue, the warrior put a seal on her shivering lips, his finger silencing the flow of details. He motioned her to place an ear on the ground below them as he picked up the mat of dog skin. Crouching beside him on the withered grass and dirt, she heard voices so loud they shook the pebbles under her earlobe.

"You got the gas line?"

"Right," answered a South Boston brogue.

"How faah ahh we hookin' it up?" asked a third.

"The Chahhles?" a fourth repeated in broad South Boston brogue.

"You're not stopping in Roxbury" the first voice asked.

Mirl's mother whispered. "In the sky—in the ground? Everything is going round."

"Shhhh, shhhhhh!" Chickatabot smoothed her wild hairs, patted her cheeks, breasts, as she clung to his rawhide pants, pointed to his eardrum. Yes, he nodded. And from another direction, they heard …

"Don' trickle that powder. Ain't nothin' up above here."

"We headed in the right direction?"

"West," sounded above the squeal of casters.

"Back Bay?"

"I thought we headed for the banks?"

• • •

"Oh, blow my baby up, babe

"Blow my baby up,

"Kingdom come, come …"

The chorus of youthful voices stopped abruptly. Fumes of gas curled through the bottom of Chickatabot's tent above.

"Hello?" asked a brogue from South Boston.

"How dee doo," answered a deep Georgia drawl.

"Who's there?"

"Who?" replied a voice from the opposite direction.

"Who?"

"O'Coogan?" whistled from the tub.

"T2?" O'Coogan sneezed after he asked.

"Don' get that pow-der in your nose, white boy. Send us all up," squeaked a juvenile general.

"Why this is duplication of effort," said O'Coogan.

"Co-rrect."

"Am I right in assuming that your penultimate destination … ?"

"Co-rrect."

"Shall we combine," offered O'Coogan.

"Absolutely," a dry peppery voice interrupted. "This is Mr. Cabbage speaking, president of the First National Massachusetts Corporation. Mr. Saltn'pepper, the board chairman, and myself, are on to your amusing schemes. It is useless to proceed in your present format. Every blade of grass is wiretapped. The greenbacks speak. However, if the two agree to burn down selected sections of the city, Roxbury, South Boston, Mattapan, Dorchester, and Charlestown, irrespective of race, religion or country of national origin, a certain sum will be left in the vaults more than sufficient to pay for their trouble. It is a waste of time to try to crack the lower safes of the banks where our major securities lie. They are wired to atomic charges and a private security force is on permanent duty there. But, as each section of Boston crumbles into ashes, another vault door will swing open and if the criminals can maintain discipline among themselves, they will have a treat.

"Mommy!" The cry quivered from Mirl's mother. The Indian suckled her breast.

Later, Chickatabot lifted his gourd to her. A liquid of crushed berries and herbs stained their cheeks, dripped down their chins. The scuttle clattered to the ground. For hours, days, weeks, with faint pulses and suspended breath—they hibernated.

The ground shook under them. Outside an orange sky bloomed. Pennants of flame announced the morning. The gas tanks in Quincy and at the lip of the Neponset in Boston exploded. O'Coogan blew all the bridges out at once, cut water, electricity, plunged even the banks into darkness. "To hell with the vaults," he sneered. "This is the last sellout."

He turned to O'Toole. "Open the sewers." As the trucks rolled down Southampton, thousands of glowering men packed into the garbage, held on to side ladders. The patricians in Back Bay and on the edge of Boston Harbor experienced a slight wooziness. The floors of their mansions and office buildings seemed unsteady, spongy, as if the soil underneath were growing marshy. Valuable parts of the city were built on land reclaimed from the tidal basins and now the water table seemed to be rising alarmingly. All wires to the municipal engineers were dead. In the gray haze of morning, in a whir of helicopters, the mayor and his staff bid their city good-bye and sailed into the rising sun. In the vaults, swimming with brine, the guards hurried down to see a mold climbing over cash, securities, eating.

In Roxbury, headquarters was delirious. The light had been getting fainter in the tub all night. The two threads had disappeared. One of the glowing black coals was out. The other blinked fitfully and ugly spots of blue, red, purple, broke out in a bruise across the surface of antibiotic.

"It's eatin' him," whispered one of the generals.

"Watch out!" A thin film of the scum lapped over the edge of the tub, seethed on the wooden floor.

Headquarters woke slowly to the pounding of fists on its closet door.

A horde of children were eagerly awaiting transport at Dudley Street Station. They had been told that the drivers were to take them in garbage and fire trucks to the vaults where wads of money would be handed out. They were dressed for a Christmas party, holding a ration of chocolate bars. The other half of the Black forces were behind the wheels of T2's rolling armor, a fleet of requisitioned Cadillacs, Continentals, Oldsmobiles, Chryslers, assembled behind Everett Square to drive out once the Celts had rounded Columbus Avenue, and push into South Boston for looting. Similarly there were no troops in Codman Square or along Talbot Avenue or Blue Hill, so as to give the white marauders from across the Neponset a free hand.

The generals explained it to the King as the last ray of green light flickered from the tub. His staff was crying but the King barked, "Stop that kid stuff. You been fooled. Call back the troops."

Too late! They heard the roar of mufflers in far off Everett Square as the Cadillacs took off; the approaching hum of the garbage and fire trucks down Dudley Street.

At the foot of Old Harbor and Columbus Avenue, a small crowd of neighborhood agitators, school committeemen, members of selected ladies auxiliaries, were awaiting the arrival of limousines to take them downtown for the first pickings in the vaults. A trifle tipsy from the bottles that were circulating, they waved happily at the El Dorados speeding right for them.

It began with a burst of automatic fire from a garbage truck.

The column had screeched to a halt under the girders of the subway, its lead vehicle drawing a bead on the eager faces.

The candy bars trembled in the children's hands. As the rattle of the clip of bullets died away in the cool morning air, there was only the rustling of torn wrappers.

"Hand grenades, Molotov cocktails, cherry bombs, land mines, handheld rockets, dynamite, poison gas, pistols, where's the pistols?"

"They all went into Southie," his staff screamed as the King ran up Warren Ave., to Dudley Street. "Crossbows, Bowie knives, straight razors, where's the straight razors?"

"Southie."

Night was about to descend through the dawn into the light, street by street, black and white … But wait!

The gates, the great gates were swinging open. A host in robes poured out of the Mattapan Insane Asylum. A multitude ran through Franklin Park.

A Chip off the Pudding

Lunatics were thundering by. Shaken to their feet, Chickatabot and his partner ran out to see. On the brow of an Indian elephant, a doctor trumpeted, "To Dudley Street."

O'Coogan escaping through the sewer pipes heard the soft pad of paws behind. "Help! Help!" cried O'Toole. Both crawled for the safety of the manhole in Brookline beyond Jamaica Pond, its waiting getaway car. There wasn't enough of O'Toole to make a meal. O'Coogan twisted around and tumbled a grenade down at the creature but the leopard knocked it back.

Outpaced by antelopes, tigers, the King fell to his knees at the corner of Warren and Townsend, began to weep. Mustapha ran by. A white lady with a handkerchief wiped the King's nose. "I'm the mop up." Far ahead at Dudley Street Station, Kezzlev's silver-haired general cackled above the tumult. The white toughs began to water in their pants. With wet breeches the black children fled. The Monkey Man's calls rang out and the dispersing mobs scratched themselves helpless.

At the western edge of the park, puddingstone quaked. From its fissure, a warrior rose, armed with the weaponry of Roman Judea. Breathing fire and volcanic ash, he strode to Blue Hill Avenue toward the corner of Talbot, where the pincer from across Neponset hurtled. A sheet of frost froze across the asphalt, trucks. Jeeps and cannon slid into one another, ramming bumpers, piling up a barricade. Ice locked the bolts and catches in the rifles, made the shimmering river behind them a solid blank across which the invading host began to back.

In midstream, a crack of doom apprehended them, set off a landslide down the face of the Great Blue in Canton miles away. The chip had been severed from its casing in conglomerate. It dashed in a boulder down the western slope, twisting up grass, pebbles, tar, cobbles, the whole of Columbia Road, sidewalks, curbs, sewer grates, tavern windows, concrete abutments, girders, the Southeast Expressway, rolling …

The most terrifying of prodigies was mere gossamer, a whisper that went through the ranks, "Seamus?"

"No?"

"Yes."

"Seamus," from one end of Boston to the other, Dorchester, Rosindale, Hyde Park, Mattapan, "Seamus." It was the quiet pad of pandemonium. "Seamus was risen from the dead."

The Cardinal's Last Stand

"Watch out, watch out!" It was too late by the time the cardinal arrived. An hour before, on the spreading green lawn of his chancery, a flying squad of bishops and the papal legate had come down.

"You clipped a finger off her!" The helicopter brushing a stone statue of the saint, hands clasped in devotion, averted catastrophe by an inch. They rushed through the back entrance of the primate's mansion.

"He's in the library," cried a housekeeper as they broke through the doors of the tan brick-and-limestone fortress, breaking glass panes in the wrought iron, splinters of it in their clothes." *Omai convien, che tu cosi ti spoltre!*" the legate called out, his Latin deserting him. "Now you must cast off all sloth!" A patriarch of Bucharest explained the line of Dante to the others, who like the cardinal lacked Italian. The ecclesiastics bundled the aging Prince of Boston into his limousine and drove into the downtown, whitewalls squealing.

Peering through the stiff white collars crowding him in the back seat, His Eminence saw men and women crying, holding hands, down on the knees, kissing the cuffs of passing trousers and hems. "*Ahi ... uomini diversi d'ogne costume e pien do'ogni magagna*, shrieked the legate. "Full of every ..." Black and white teenagers were feeding each other clusters of purple grapes on Tremont. "*Perche no siete voi del mondo spersi?*" Why are you not driven from the world?" The cardinal did not believe he was in Boston.

There was no traffic in the streets but the Cadillac had to swerve crossing Washington Street to avoid a loping camel in the narrow thoroughfare. Three boys between its humps were showering peanuts on pedestrians, who knelt in attitudes of worship on the sidewalks. House and shop doors were thrown open. A persistent chanting drowned out the cry of the cleric driving. "Stop the music," he shouted out the window. The car slowed to a crawl in a procession choking Massachusetts Avenue, Harrison and Albany Street, moving towards Boston City Hospital.

Squeezing through the crowd, carried by two burly Jesuits, in his wheelchair, the cardinal and the ecclesiastics reached the hospital's doors, but the entryway, packed with smiling faces, would hardly give an inch. The line in front of the elevators was endless. It would be hours before they could get up to the seventh floor. The arms reaching out to embrace them were making the bishops nervous. "Maybe we should get out of here?" suggested one.

"*S' io fossi pur di tanto ancor leggero/ ch'i' potessi in cent'anni andare un'oncia* . . . if I were yet so light, that I could in a hundred years, go an inch ..." but at that the Rumanian disappeared and so did the Jesuits. The legate twisted nervously beside the cardinal for a few moments; then glided away in the throng, tearful, surreptitiously throwing a kiss behind him.

"Your Eminence?"

Despite the sweet hum in the corridor and stairway shaft a familiar voice sounded in the prelate's ear. "McShane?" barked the cardinal.

"Yes sir."

"What are you doing?"

"The same old thing."

"The same old thing?"

"Telling stories …"

"The same stories?"

"No, Your Eminence. A few new ones."

Slowly the people in front of the wheelchair began to part and it rolled forward a few feet toward an elevator, miraculously empty.

"I thought I kicked you out of Boston?"

"You did."

"You were an atheist," the cardinal mumbled.

"Agnostic, sir, a pagan agnostic."

"But the boys set you up in the park?"

"Yes, sir."

"Right under my nose?"

"Yes, sir."

"There's no faith in the world."

The elevator rose to the seventh floor. As the metal doors rolled open and the cardinal wheeled himself out, the light was blinding. "Turn off the floods," he called. "None of yer tricks."

"It's me," said McShane, his sweet voice echoing from a room at the far end of the corridor. "I'm sorry. You'll get used to it in a while."

"How did this happen?"

"I was talking to some Jews."

"Hebes."

"That's one of the nicknames."

"That tribe that lived on Blue Hill Avenue?"

"Aye."

"I thought they all moved out of there?"

"These two stayed behind, or below, so to speak."

"How did you get in with them?" asked the Cardinal.

"I was listening to their stories."

"You always was a sucker for a good one. How come you're shinin' so?"

"Fish."

"Don't try to make me believe you're a fish, McShane."

"No, sir. It's only the scales."

"What scales?"

"Leviathan, sir. Just a spot or two—the old worm of the deep."

"How did you come by that?"

"Talking to those Jews, sir."

"I never encountered such conversation with that tribe. I've known some of them close as family. All the talk I ever got out of them was dollars and cents. I suspected the whole bunch was atheists, or Communists on the sly." The cardinal was wheeling slowly forward into the hot glow. "How old were these Hebes?"

"Two thousand years or so."

"That might explain it," said His Eminence, squinting carefully, turning his chair to face the room where the voices were coming from. "Would you turn down the lights, McShane?"

"I know it would be a great mercy to you sir. But if you squinny a moment or two more, maybe it won't seem quite so luminous."

"It's burning my cheeks and I want to get closer."

"Think of it as a bit of a suntan."

"The same old wiseguy, McShane?"

"The same, sir."

"Oh, you're an awful trickster. I can feel the heat of you even if I can't see you straight."

"I notice you are inching up," the officer remarked.

"It's your own light, is it?"

"Oh no, borrowed. A lending."

"I came to see you once or twice, before, but …"

"I saw."

"You was indisposed."

"Between heaven and earth."

The cardinal creaked uncomfortably in his wheelchair. He had forced himself to within a foot of Seamus' door. "Exactly what are you up to?"

"A sentimental journey," the officer replied.

"How long?"

"At this moment, it's not up to me."

"Are you aware of what is going on outside?"

"Topsy-turvy?"

"As you say," growled His Eminence.

"I'd like to see it."

"It's upset the Higher-ups."

"Always will."

"Am I almost up to you?"

"A few more feet."

"How about the heat?"

"It's one with the illumination," Seamus apologized.

"Aren't you uncomfortable?"

"Not at all. I feel only bliss."

The cardinal's hands fanned the air. It was hot as a furnace. The smell of brimstone, he thought, carefully concealed in an ointment of cloves and some deodorant. "Can I touch you?"

"Why not?"

"It won't burn?"

"I can't tell. I'm feeling cool as a cucumber. It's all in the face of the beholder."

The cardinal's hand struck a knee not his own. "Is that you?"

"You bet."

His Eminence leaned forward, reached out again and touched the cloth of a hospital gown. "Still you?"

"The same."

"I begin to perceive you."

"What do I look like?"

"Just a flitting impression. Too bright to really say."

"Sir, it's the same ugly mug."

"No, no, something isn't quite the same. More striking I would say. Even alluring. I wish I could see your toes."

"Sir?"

"Is this the chin?"

"Ay."

"The nose?"

The sound of assent no sooner out of the officer's mouth, the cardinal shuffled his sleeve so a pair of silver gongs fell into his fingers and seizing Seamus by the nostrils, clapped it over their flaring tips. The cleric crying, "Come off! Off! You child of Lucifer!" pulled for all he was worth—and called out, "In the name of Saint Dunstan!"

The shout of the policeman, more surprise than pain, rattled the bed slats. He leaned over, before His Eminence shouting could do more damage and gave him a hard box on the ear.

The old man staggered back into his wheelchair. His head was ringing. "Am I hearing angels?" he asked aloud.

"Not this time. I'm sorry, sir, but you've still got the strength of Satan in your fingers. Not to mention the nutcracker."

"Satan!" the cardinal whistled, cocking his red cap. "So that nose is yours?"

"Whose would it be but my own?"

"I was hoping … Satan, you know, is an old hand at disguises."

"Is that so?"

"I'm not ashamed to say, I've stolen a trick or two at times out of Lucifer's handbook."

"I've seen."

"Don't glare at me so harshly, Officer McShane."

"Certainly not. Despite our differences, I've always entertained the deepest respect for Your Eminence."

"I was only doing my job."

"I understand."

"This unusual aura of yours puts me in a pretty pickle."

"How so?"

"I was hurried out of my house and hustled into Boston to put out a fire in a Christmas tree. They were all quiet when that demented priest was rampaging about, abusing Jews, but now the Higher-ups have smelled real smoke and I was supposed to stamp you out."

"Sir, I'll resent another liberty upon my person, toe or fingers."

"No chance of that Seamus, if an old man may be permitted to be familiar. I'm convinced."

"Well?"

"Well …" The cardinal pulled his cap to the very back of his scalp and peered into the blaze of glory trying to distinguish the features of McShane's face. "I …"

"Yes."

"I … I'm ancient. I know, the legs won't carry me. The jig is up. Still, Seamus, some of the timeworn slogans must still hold a drop. I know 'em all. I'm … '*Caritas*,' isn't that still good? '*Caritas*,' Seamus?"

"Aye."

"I knew it. One of my favorites. Always good on the tongue, a peppermint each time I pronounced it over a hopeless situation. '*Caritas*,' Seamus, sir, I'm not used to …"

"To?"

"Unemployment."

"Sir?" asked the officer.

"Couldn't you use me?"

"How?"

"Spreading the word."

"As far as I know there is no money involved in me making my appearance."

"I …"

"There's no hierarchy."

"I …"

"Not even an advance man."

"I know a bit about that. After all I took a vow of poverty."

"No church dormitories …"

"A crust, a crumb …"

"I don't know anything about money."

"Seamus, forget I even alluded to it. I put a bit by. All I want is your assurance I wouldn't be annoying you."

"Not a chance of it, Your Eminence."

"It's a great blessing, you've put upon me."

"Are you sure you have the doctrine straight?"

"I'll stick to '*Caritas*.' I don't want to be wasting your time," said the cardinal, his hand on the wheel of his chair.

"It's a bit more complicated than that."

"Aye?"

"It goes back about four thousand years, a lot of books. I'm just getting the hang of it myself."

"I'm no good at that. I never really had the Latin. All the history and argument is just a buzzing in my ears. *Caritas*, aye?"

"You won't be adding anything else?" the officer asked.

"No."

"Not making up a few rules on your own to enforce the idea?"

"Never."

"Or an efficient collection system to get the '*Caritas*' around?"

"Me word."

"No hokey pokey."

"Absolutely not."

"A business suit or whatever is appropriate in the area you're passing through so as not to attract any eye-catching attention?"

The cardinal clapped his cap off his skull in amazement. "Are you on to me?"

"I am. It's the fault of the o'er dazzling radiance, none of my own doing. It shines right into every nook and cranny of your brain and reels off the answers before I get the questions up. I tell you, Your Eminence, it's too much for the world, and I'm not long for it now." Seamus took the cleric's crabbed hands in his own and kissed their knuckles. "I envy you, Your Eminence."

"How's that?" asked the latter, meekly.

"Watch out for panthers. I hear the flies are something fierce. Man-eating fish, poisoned arrows, and a fistful of plagues. Better get yourself inoculated. One favor I want from you in particular."

"Certainly."

"If one of the little ladies offers, as I'm sure she will, seeing that even in your crippled state, you have a fine profile and full head of handsome white hair—comfort in the flesh—"

"I …"

The beams of the officer's face stoked the fiery blush of the cardinal's. Licks of fire started from the latter's hoary nostril hairs. "In return," continued McShane, drowning out his protest. "For your spiritual tender. It would be a personal favor to me if you would overcome your former scruples and take it. If you have any trouble, or hesitation, all you have to do is say your single, three-syllable creed aloud in the act, '*Caritas.*'"

"'*Caritas?*'"

"Ay, '*Caritas.*' And your understanding of the same will be happily improved."

"Am I to understand this as a point of doctrine?"

"Absolutely."

"A kind of communion?"

"One word is all I will allow you from the old vocabulary," the officer cautioned, '*Caritas.*'"

The cardinal began to cry. "'Tis awful hard on an old man like me."

"I know. I know." McShane patted his hands.

"How about all those middle aged …"

"Two wrongs don't make a right."

"Sure and that's so," said the man slumped in his wheelchair, blinking through his tears. "May I repeat that."

"I wouldn't mind."

"Could I ask, not to be impertinent, whose mouth you heard that from?"

"My mother's."

"So the Hebrews don't have a monopoly?"

"Certainly not."

"No?"

"They never said they did."

"That's a blessing."

The figure of the officer in the bed shook his head.

"I know," the cleric piped in an undertone. "It's a new ball game. '*Caritas*,' is all I ask, sir. I'll get the hang of the new rules. '*Caritas*.'"

"Off with you now, Your Eminence, I feel as if I'm fading."

The light in the room was no less but the body that the cardinal could distinguish in the bed, upright, seemed less substantial than before. "A last favor?"

"What's that?"

"I wonder …" The elder man shifted his crippled bones, uneasy under his ecclesiastical gown. "Couldn't …" He looked at the floor. "Not a total resurrection." He cleared his throat, feeling a stare of disapproval. "A bit more spring, perhaps …" His gaze wandered up but he could not face the brightness directly. "Lame in the legs, of course, but upright?"

"No more miracles," came the answer.

"No more?"

"None. The memory of me won't be with you long. Tomorrow all the history of the horse and me will be forgotten. Stick by your creed, '*Caritas*.' "

"Just '*Caritas*'?"

The last words His Eminence heard before the figure faded from the room haunted him after, set him on the road he was to follow, "A little self-*Caritas* will work miracles Your Eminence."

Utopia

U topia. **Create Utopia**, a world for the Messiah, to tempt Messiah. What better Utopia than the last pages of a romance? What is a romance but a small utopia? Tying up of loose ends happily, ever after, a better world. One turns to the pages of one's own life, to the tune of the Chilean poet, "*À l'aurore, armés d'une ardente patience, nous entrerons aux splendides Villes.*" (In the dawn, armed with a burning patience, we shall enter the splendid cities.)

Tie the knots together in a town now splendid, "*splendida esplendida*," conquered by poetry, by miles of grass and trees, as block by block, it recovers the smell of fir, pine and leaves. Spread this parkland a green canvas right and left, a coverlet of jonquils, dandelions, freckled lilies over the smoking streets, a coat of many colors. Boston bedecked in park. A corner of emerald touches the Atlantic unbroken by asphalt. Another weds the Neponset River, the Charles. Its flanks are washed by three waters.

Greensward swallows up the asphalt, buckles the cobbles in every other street. Brooks gurgle up pallid from sewer pipes, rill between the city's streams, making the margins of wide-skirted meads.

Festooned with Corinthians, curling in Ionic, the columns of a noble house here and there survive—even an occasional triple-decker which time has solaced with grape and ivy vine. The snake slithers over rusting automobiles and onions rattle the engine valves.

The city preserves a history of childhood, the Messiah's garden. We call it Utopia.

Utopia, romance—what is conventional romance without a marriage? One? Have another and another, who's counting?

As his army of elephants faded into clouds again, Kezzlev found himself with a crowd of dazed patients and doctors, bewildered children, hungover garbagemen, truck drivers and teenagers, at a street crossing in Roxbury. Chochom was heading back for a Thanksgiving service in Franklin Park, when standing on a boulder of conglomerate over the trolley tracks girding Seaver Street, was the rabbi's wife looking left, right. "Mrs. Ostropol, I presume?"

"Yes."

"I was hoping, we?"

"*We* what?"

"We could take a walk."

"Why?"

"Why not?"

"I'm married."

"Married?" the doctor asked, "but …"

"But what?"

"Your husband …

"Yes?"

The doctor's mouth rustled with dry grass. "I saw … the sky."

"I …" Rochelle struggled with words but tears broke into her speech. "The sky … I … why? Angels, tricks! Running away from me? I'm awake."

"It's true," whistled the little man. "He's in the blue." They wept, together, the leopard tugging at the doctor's pant leg. "Shahh, shah," whispered the doctor, patting the snarling head, "Everything's all right." And then to her, "Hold tight."

"Running away!" Rochelle broke from the doctor's grasp. "Always running. From the kitchen, bedroom, study. Never helped. The dishes? Wouldn't stay in *shul*." Running behind her into the park, the doctor, leopard, a train of kids pursued the rabbi's wife. "He never helped."

"Messiah!" called the voices, "a Messiah!"

"Messiah?" Rochelle wheeled. "Not to flush the toilet. Hide under the bed. Cheat at Harvard. Plagiarize, make up, *mishigass*, all *mishgass*."

"Yes, yes!"

"He couldn't …"

"Up, up," their voices redounded off the blue vault of Boston skies. A faint yellow band diffused through the azure color—the gleam off a wedding band. "Look!"

"Rochelle," whistled through the lindens. "Rochelle, Rochelle." A single star of moist frond flew in the breeze and pasted itself to her cheek.

"Enough!" the doctor resumed his hold on her hand. "No more miracles. It's up to us. Maishe is no more."

"How do I know?"

"Did anyone go looking for Moses on Mount Nebo? I came here to find blessings, exchange a word, a whisper. It didn't work." He paused. "Say, why don't we take a walk?"

"Okay," she wiped her tears.

"Okay," beamed the doctor."

"How did you know my name?" the lady asked shyly.

"The whole of Boston has been talking, asking, where's the wife, the rabbi's wife?"

"Not the rabbi?"

"You are asking. I am asking, where's the rabbi?" sighed the doctor. "In the sky? Witnesses?" He shook his head. "No. When you disappeared—rape, kidnapping—everyone wants to know. Blacks? Whites? Right here in Franklin Park? Into the newspapers, a million calls a day. Everyone with something to say: "I did it … he did it … she did it." Theories, eyewitness reports, a bond rally—" the doctor went on and on. Astonished, the rabbi's wife opened her mouth.

Such pretty lips, thought Chochom, and before he could stop himself, he had put his own to them.

A sharp slap clipped his face, tongue. "I don't like that." He choked. She took his hand, "You behave, I'll behave. You want to talk, okay. The other thing is *traif* until I get a ruling. No touching, tickling, just talk. Talk, talk, talk or I'm taking off."

"T … t … talk. Talk is fine with me. I love talk …" As they strode about the park, Chochom's voice tripped on. "I'll talk, sing, pray."

"No," she cut him short, "Dangerous. You're not a Messiah?"

"Only a doctor," cried Kezzlev. The train behind him called. "*Sist nur ein Arzt. Sist nur ein Arzt.*"

"You saw him?"

Kezzlev began to cry. "Yes, yes," he confessed. "I told you. I'll lose you."

"Me too," she whispered, squeezing his fingers. "But *you'll* stay on the ground."

"Yes."

"I want babies. Real babies. Flesh and blood. My babies. Babies."

"All right," said Chochom. "I'm ready."

"What's your name?" she asked, blowing her nose into a handkerchief.

"Chochom."

"You're not a rabbi?"

"Only a doctor."

A voice bellowed. "No more doctors."

On top of Hagborne Hill stood a lady, breasts falling out of her dress. "Enough with the doctors." A red man beside her wagged his head up and down.

"I'm not practicing," Chochom called.

"What are you doing?"

"Giving legal counsel."

"Stick to the facts," Rochelle said.

"You and me," he replied, hugging her.

"Mummy!" Over the hills of Franklin Park, from Hagborne, Schoolmaster, Scarboro, Rock Morton, the call rattled bones in the earth, shook the trees. "Mummy, Mummy!"

From the charred roof of the old refectory, above the blunted angels' faces carved into masonry, "Mummy, Mummy!" Above the ruined pilasters, Doric columns, shadows long on the broken, grassy terrace, fragments of frieze, a band of women in robes of silver, faces fresh as snow, the coal black King among them, one woman waved, calling, "Mummy, Mummy!"

A peal rang out from Hagborne, a cannonball, sucked into, out of the lungs of her mother, one, two, three, it burst over Nazingdale, "Mirl, Mirl, Mirl!"

Mother, daughter, brides, grooms, what kisses, embraces, savage couplings to record; pen cannot scratch, dig deep enough into paper. It is inscribed in gray-green rock thick with purple veins and chalky palms of stone, the taffy of ages before the ice cap. Take it between your teeth, almond brittle of tears, chocolate, nuts, honey out of the rock, the fat of this moment.

Everyone is about to get married.

• • •

All through the hamlets of the Hub, the sound of singing rises from the bride's couch. "Through the impulse from below there is a stirring above, and through the impulse from above there is a stirring higher up still, until the impulse reaches the place where the lamp is to be lit and is lit." So speaks the blessed Zohar.

THE LAMP IS LIT. What is Utopia but a return to Eden? What is Eden but a metaphor for a mystical union between man and the Ultimate Mystery? What do we know of union on earth, the lowest, the highest? One turns over on top of the other and we are rolled away.

Tom-toms and wood flutes enfold Mirl's mother in the skins of the last of the Ponkapoags, the archer Chickatabot. The hand of the King of Blue Hill, a descendant of Keturah and Abraham, is knotted in the shy palm of Mirl. The children of the sixties will create an original commonwealth. Mustapha has a last chance for sanctity with *our lady of the shopping bags*.

The final knot—forty days, forty nights, the citizens searched each crack and crevice of Franklin Park with lights, picks, shovels. Mustapha's wife was the last eyewitness and she swore Maishe had hopped the wall just past the corner of Blue Hill and Seaver. Not a bone, or set of dentures was recovered. According to the strictly Orthodox, no one could testify that Rochelle Ostropol was a widow. Still, deep in the cistern system channeled out of puddingstone through the western swells of Franklin Park, the shreds of a black rabbinical suit were found, lapel threads peculiar to a tailor who had outfitted the rabbi since infancy.

Rochelle consented to take the hand of Kezzlev.

As for Fletcher, the keeper, he had lived too long with beasts to accommodate himself to the ferocity of the opposite sex. Instead, he was persuaded to run for mayor of the new municipality. "Man is a political animal," as the philosopher Aristotle said. "This man knows animals."

It was His Eminence's last endorsement, the first public one, before leaving in his wheelchair for South America. He had called Rome and tried to persuade an old friend to come along but the latter protested, "What about all those middle-aged Catholics."

"Too late," sighed the Boston cleric, putting the receiver down. "Would have been fun."

Along the damp equatorial paths of South American jungles, his wheelchair slithering over serpents, glides His Eminence floating on pontoons across dangerous fords, attended by a school of natives trailing infants with the pug noses of Kerry, hair red, black and blond, naked, singing "Toora Loora, Loora."

Kezzlev set up a center for spiritual studies in the old Franklin Park refectory. Many strolling at the doctor's heels lost themselves along side trails, gardens, finding a sympathetic partner in a bower of flowers, evergreens. Others on the foundation stones of the old Monkey House sat in moonlight discussing the terms of the Holy One's marriage through man and woman.

Seamus and the sod, shriveled to a few grains of dust, blew out the windows of the hospital. Many years later a man appeared in a waving surgical gown through the counties of Ireland preaching "*Caritas*" and reintroducing the snake in the grass.

Far off on the other side of the continent, S. J. O'Halloran set up as the anti-Pope. In the shock of the assault, he had lost his English and spoke to Los Angeles only in the silver of Church Latin. Draw, draw, drink at "the musk rose full of dewy wine." The doctor and the rabbi's wife are on the couch. The latter uncovers herself, "O that his left hand were under my head and that his right hand would embrace me." Above them a voice calls, "I am Black but beautiful," below them, "D … D … Don't stop. D … D … Don't." "For the lower waters flow forth to meet the upper." All over Dorchester, Roxbury, Mattapan, the smoke goes up from the mattresses. "The lamp is kindled above and all are blessed from it."

Peace, what peace. This is "the true, the blissful" cup of plenty, "beaded bubbles winking at the brim."

All is content, quiet, harmony, agreement, prayer, song, and incense.

Except for one band of cynics, "old believers" sticking by the sour conviction in a tiny ghetto that the Messiah is a long way off. As far as they are concerned the whole story is full of holes. Rochelle's consenting to take Kezzlev's hand is adultery. And even if it is a *bubbemeiser* is this tale fair to Rachel, the little girl in pigtails who followed Maishe? How about her dreams? Why introduce the Black queen into the story, have her steal Rachel's groom? In the Holy Script Rachel has to wait for her sister. In the stories which are as old as the script itself, Rachel lay under the bed giving the latter instructions on her own wedding night. Kezzlev is a consolation prize. It is Maishe, Rochelle wants.

Even if Ostropol is not a Messiah, not even a real rabbi, he understands more than this faker, Kezzlev. For Maishe wanted something beyond the household gods, some ineffable spirit of eroticism and knowledge that will ... But, frankly, the young man never made himself clear and the tale trailed into abstractions. Could the Black queen really be an aspect of Rachel? There is a way to solve this, but not in this century. Centuries past, the text is hinting, an attempt was made. Maybe centuries hence?

Let's not pretend. Marriage is a consolation prize. All our blissful matches are temporary patches, while we hope for the supreme union with the Unknown who will satisfy all cravings, fantasies, twist us into endless kinks.

Sedulous publications originate from this band, slips of paper tacked on door fronts, stuffed in Utopia's mailboxes, "Isn't it boring?"

```
Really happy? That's happi-
ness?
Get a lick of Leviathan?
Did Death go away? Say?
Send $10.00 c/o More in Store
```

In the field house, the refectory, where the doctor had his headquarters and sent forth the word which civilized so many, they have the book of personal testimonies, the handbook of morning, afternoon, and evening prayers: but the sect stubbornly refuses any compromises.

None of their members saw the miracles. They acknowledge that the new doctrine has improved some people's way of life. Natural disasters certainly occurred. Still that is not it, no. They're sorry.

"It is something else that is promised. Something quite different, after all."

Nose V

Is love the will to Messiah, the tale of a world uplifted? Joshua the son of Nun sent two spies to look at the Promised Land. They lodged at a whore's house, Rachab's in Jericho. Report of this delving reached the King of Jericho. *"Bring me those men!"*

"They came but went just now—hurry after!" Rachab answered. But she had hidden them on her roof under stalks of flax. To the Jordan's ford the king's men sped while the gate shut behind them. Up on the roof, Rachab whispered, *"I know that the Lord has given the land to you. Because terror of you is fallen upon us—the inhabitants of the land faint before you. We heard how the Lord dried up the waters of the Red Sea before you in your going out of Egypt. And what you did to the two kings of the Amorites that were across the Jordan, to Sihon and Og, how you religiously wiped them out. We heard, and our hearts melted. And it does not stand*

up anymore, the spirit in a man before you. Because the Lord your God, he is God in heaven above and in earth below. And now, swear to me, please by God, since I have done a kindness to you, you will also do so to my father's house. Give me a true sign."

Rachab saved her father's house, sisters', the whole family. Our spies told her, after she let them down from her house on the town wall, *"Show the scarlet cord on which we hung. Bind it from the window."*

The red tassel! The rabbis flocked to her place. Rachab became a pious proselyte. Talmud Bavli, Zabahim, 116a: *"And Rachab the whore too said to Joshua's spies, 'Because we heard how the Lord dried up the waters of the Red Sea.'"*

Why say, *"There was not any more spirit in them before the Children of Israel,"* in *Joshua* 5:1, and in *Joshua* 2:11 hint, *"And it does not stand up [Komoh] anymore, the spirit in a man before you"?* Rachab meant that the Canaanites could not make their pricks kick.

"And how did she know this? A master said, 'There was no prince or ruler who had not *shtouped* Rachab the whore. It was said, She was ten years old when the Israelites departed from Egypt, and she played the whore the whole of the forty years spent by the Israelites in the wilderness. At the age of fifty she became a proselyte. Said she, 'May I be forgiven as a reward for the cord, the window, and the flax.'"

The rabbis pun—their hands on every dot in the text. The Hebrew word *komoh* can mean "remain" or "stand." The rabbis note the parallel expressions in nearby passages of Joshua. *"All the kings of the Amorites which were on the side of the Jordan westward, and all the kings of Canaanites which were by the sea,"* had *"no spirit in them."* They hear Rachab repeat, *"It does not stand up anymore, the spirit in a man."* They ask, "How does a prostitute know what is privy only to the Holy One, blessed be He?" They squeezed the text. Rachab said the *spirit* wasn't *standing up,* in any man. She was lying with, sitting on every king among the Amorites and Canaanites. Soft with terror, his highness couldn't "*stand up.*" Rachab inspired, rose when the kings fell.

Rachab was an expert on "*spirit.*" Spirit and seed are synonymous in this passage of Talmud. There is an opinion that Rachab's foreknowledge came because the Divine Spirit rested on her. The waters of spirit are deep. Megillah 15a: *"They taught, our Rabbis—the four most beautiful women in the world were who? Sarah, Abigail, Rachab, and Esther.* (One sage says Esther was a bit green, sallow. Substitute instead, her rival, Vashti.) *Rachab through her name, caused lust, Jael through her voice,*

Abigail through her memory, Michal, daughter of Saul, through appearance.

"Said Rabbi Isaac, 'Whoever says her name aloud, "Rachab, Rachab," immediately has a spurt of sperm.'

"Rabbi Nachman replied, 'I just said, "Rachab, Rachab!" Nothing happens?'

"Rabbi Isaac replied, 'I speak only of one who knew her intimately. Through her name he sees her again.'"

"Rachab! Rachab!" Rabbi Isaac whispers. His face is hot. His cheeks are red. He stirs, flies and falls under his garment. He imagines and becomes intimate, taking a place at her side.

The sound is enough to draw out the wisest. Doubt the act is sacred? The Talmud repeats the story in Ta'anith 5b. Why?

Hebrew linguistics pronounce "*Rachab*," which means in Hebrew, "wide, broad, spacious" (the *ch* or *h* like clearing the top of the throat of flame, *chi*). The rule of metathesis: which is the misplacement of sounds within a word through the hard usage of time. So the English insect of brilliant wings, the "flutterby" became the absurd "butterfly" and the original "cruls" of thy hair became "curls." Edward Horowitz: "Hebrew is a very ancient language having a history going back thousands of years. During by far the greatest part of this time there was no printing and so large numbers of words are current in two forms: the original correct form and a metathesized one … In the largest number of examples of metathesis in Hebrew, not the faintest difference in meaning exists between the two forms of the word."

Flip the "ch" of "*Rachab*" ("b" and "v" are designated by a common letter, *bays* or *vays*, in Hebrew) and we have an old friend, "*ravach*," also meaning to be wide, spacious, to give relief (Brown Driver Briggs *Gesenius*).

Rachab between the age of ten and fifty slept with all the kings of the Middle East. She gave relief to the great men of the world. No wonder she was called, "Relief." It was such a crowd that she acquired the other meaning of the word, "spacious" or "roomy." In Arabic, the root of *Rachab* means "wide between the thighs."

This is the pun that Rabbi Nachman appreciated as he spoke the syllables and strained after "relief." If he did not disappear into the holy space, it was only because he could not smell Rachab. Smell—the nose of Messiah. The root of *Rachab* is related also to *rayach*. Hebrew linguistics is metaphysics. Horowitz: "*Ruach*—wind, breath. The wind is not only one of the great primal forces on this earth but it is invisible as well. When a person died, one of the most striking things noted was that his breath left him: and so the Hebrews anciently used the word *ruach* to mean 'spirit,' that which combined power and invisibility. The space between any two things is essentially the empty air that lies between them. So a slightly changed form of *ruach*, namely *ravach* came to mean 'space' and the verb *rovach* means 'to be wide, spacious.' When you have plenty of space, you are comfortable and relieved ... Coming from *ruach* is *rayach*, meaning a smell or a fragrance which is carried by the wind. *Ruach* leads us to the *Ruach Kodosh*, the Holy One, Spirit, blessed be He ..."

The breath of divinity blows through the ecstasy of Rachab's name. From the land of Sheba, Isaiah promises that in the days of Messiah, incense shall come, the smell, the taste, the sensation of ... Rachab?

Many rabbis, jealous then and now, blame Joshua for marrying her. See Megillah 14b. Either they ignore the eight prophets descended from this union: Neriah, Baruch, Serayah, Mahsetya, Jeremiah, Hilkiah, Manamel, and Shallum: the seven kings, and the prophetess Hulda—from whom we received the five books of Moses again, for it was she who told King Josiah the lost text was authentic. Angry sages crowd into the streets of Jerusalem to call Huldah's cousin, Jeremiah, "a son of a whore." Jeering, they hoot—because the spies allowed Rachab to carry her enormous brood out of Jericho to escape that city's destruction, her descendent Jeremiah had to prophesy destruction—the Temple's.

Sour grapes.

The space between the thighs of Rachab is filled with light. The spies who came to visit Rachab were no other than the children of Tamar, Perez, and Zerah: seeds, joy, squeezed from the union of father and daughter-in-law. The hand of Zerah comes out first. Around it the midwife tied a fillet of red. Though Perez over-came his brother and rolled first into the world, in the position of eldest was Zerah. Zerah—Zohar—light. It means shine forth, brightness, splendor.

O mystical text, the Zohar! O Shining! The fil-let tied to Zerah's finger, a red ribbon, was the token he gave to Rachab. She hung it from her window to signal the Hebrew armies to spare her house: the scarlet ribbon, token of her light. "Open your doors." Rachab, her name means roomy—divine light has room for all. All man may share in Rachab, Joshua's bride, taste of a messianic union, mother of kings and prophets. Will Messiah introduce a fellowship of ecstasy? This is the dread doctrine of a Torah, Law, of permitted, not forbidden, acts.

• • •

The Messiah and the Black queen? It's an old story. I didn't start it. Our fathers, Abraham, Judah, our teacher, Moses, our judge, Joshua, all heard of it.

"Free the feminine divine power from the power of the devil, the world will be perfect."

In a night crisscrossed with falling stars, of girls, trembling in the cups of their under-garments, sitting and rising and sitting again, I heard of the captivation of the Holy One, in the guise of a female, through a flaw, a crack, a holy infinitesimal split that widened out from its hair breadth at the moment of creation until it assumed the dimensions of a flaw, an indepen-dent existence. "There was a crisis in the divine world, somewhere in creation. From that crisis emerged—evil which became independent, began the struggle against the divine power. The devil has gotten a foothold in the divine world. This is the cause of the exile of the Jews, a part of God is under the yoke of the devil."

The texts, which first spoke of it have all crumbled into air, fire, water. The female pres-ence of the Holy One rests upon a man until he groans—his soul entangled in spirit as perfume. But woman, the very principle of the female, as it shudders in the Divine, the holiness, as being "captivated by the devil," is something new. It is the unquiet formulation of a thirteenth-century Kabbalist, Rabbi Isaac Ha-Cohen, toiling to find the Holy One, grasping the mystery as Her, then feeling Her slip away. Entangled in the tail of the demonic powers of the Universe, an oily film swirled in the rocks and crannies of the Span-ish mountains, awaiting the day when through cosmic explosion its nature would be trans-formed, refined. Everything hinged, Rabbi Isaac realized, on the future. Man must bend himself to the holy task, the rescue!

From this doctrine of Rabbi Isaac Ha-Cohen, contemporaries, relatives, family, son-in-laws, famous commentators, fled: do repeat a word of it.

Curdled in forgotten vellum, in a resin of myrrh, a stain dripping down the parchment, a translucent smudge on a window of the night, is the thumbprint of Rabbi Isaac. It waited for the eye of another Isaac, the holy lion, Ari, Isaac Ha-Luria, who set fire to the oil, from his bowls on the hilltops of Sfad, a fire of incense to summon the bride, the captive bride.

Is this trapped feminine power the bride? The bride of Messiah? Who was the bride of the son of David, the Messianic prototype? Did she not lament in Solomon's song, *"O kiss me, kiss me. I am in the doorway, my beloved. Kiss me with the kisses of your mouth. Kiss me."*

• • •

Is Sheba an African lady, the Shulamite? Are the tents of Kedar white? Swarthy goatskins are pitched by the Bedouins outside Beersheba. Even the Midrash Rabba (I.5) admits, *"As the tents of Kedar* (The Song of Songs 1:5), just as the tents of Kedar, although from outside they look ugly, black, and ragged, yet inside contain precious stones and pearls, so,"* etc. But

Solomon who knew more about black than the sages sang:

> *I am dark but comely*
> *O daughters of Jerusalem*
> *Like the tents of Kedar,*
> *Like the pavilions of Solomon.*
> *Do not stare at me because I am swarthy*
> *Because the sun has gazed upon me.*

Why black like *the pavilions of Solomon*? Josephus: "Now Solomon had a divine sagacity in all things, and was very diligent and studious to have things done after an elegant manner: so he did not neglect the care of the ways, but he laid a causeway of black stone along the roads that led to Jerusalem, which was the royal city, both to render them easy for travelers and to manifest the grandeur of his riches and government." On such a pavilion of black stones, or black checkered with white, the sun poured down on the "middle of the court that was before the house of the Lord" on the day that Solomon hallowed the Temple. Gaster: "That pavilion was regarded as a kind of 'sun trap'—an earthly bode by residing in which the god might be saved from the darkling regions below. This interpretation is … proved by the actual orientation of the Temple. Its entrance faced directly toward the summit of the Mount of Olives. Now, it is above that summit that the sun rises at or about the time of the autumnal equinox, so that its rays would then pour down directly upon the altar, as a kind of solar theophany!" Forget the trap, the darkling regions below, but imagine the sun pouring over Shlomo the king. His girlfriend was black, his causeways, black, his pavilions flooded with a darkening sun. Solomon spoke in images—tents, complexions, pavilions.

Messiah and the Black queen. Moses married a lady from Cush?

The family saw a black lady. Yelling, screaming, carrying on. Threats—excommunication. You would think they were speaking in the name of the Holy One, blessed be He. That's what they thought.

And Miriam and Aaron spoke against Moses because of the Cushite woman whom he had married: for he had married a Cushite woman. And they said: "Had the Lord indeed spoken only with Moses? Has He not spoke also with us?" And the Lord heard it …

And the anger of the Lord was hot against them; and He departed. And when the cloud was removed from over the Tent, look—Miriam was leprous, white as snow; and Aaron turned to Miriam, and look, she was leprous.

And Aaron said unto Moses: "Oh my lord, lay not, please, sin upon us, because we have been foolish and have sinned. Let her not, please, be as one dead, who comes out the womb of his mother and his flesh is half eaten." And Moses cried to the Lord, saying: "O God, please, heal, please, her." And the Lord said to Moses: "If her father had spit, spit in her face, should she not be ashamed seven days. Let her be shut up, outside the camp seven days, and after that brought in again." (Numbers 12:1-14).

The nose on your face turns leprous white. The Lord speaks in "similitudes" to Aaron and Miriam (but not to Moses). White in its absolute is not purity but as Aaron cries, seeing Miriam leprous, *"flesh … half eaten … as one dead."*

This is the method of the Holy Writ. Cassuto: "Semitic thought avoids general statements. Particularly in the case of a book like ours, which was not intended for thinkers and the elect few only, but for the people, it was proper that its ideas should be embodied in the language of concrete description."

If Miriam the prophetess had a hard time with the truth, her descendants squirmed in front of the text. Talmud: Moed Katan, 16b: "Was she a Cushite—the wife of Moses? Was not her name Zipporah? But as a Cushite woman is distinguishable by her skin so was also Zipporah distinguished by her deeds." A tale follows. The Cushite woman is really Zipporah and the spat has to do with the fact that Moses separated from her, had no marital relations when the Divine Presence came down on him … The number of sages who put their names to this is depressing but Joseph Kaspi, a medieval commentator, exclaimed:

I am surprised at the ancients, who are so much more perfect than me, to the soles of whose feet I do not reach, how it ever occurred to them to explain a text in the Torah the very reverse of its written meaning ... What was Onkelos' warrant for rendering the Hebrew adjective Kushit (Black or Ethiopian) 'beautiful,' the very opposite to white. Furthermore, what warrant had he for adding that 'he had deserted or separated himself from the beautiful woman that he had taken?' If that had been the intention of the text why did it not say so in so many words? Why was the exact reverse recorded? Moreover, who gave us license to tamper so with the text? Where was Onkelos' authority to do such a thing? Or the sages of the Talmud or Ibn Ezra, all of whom agreed to this explanation? Why shouldn't we do the same thing, each one doing what is right in his own eyes, till we amend the text '*Thou shalt love the Lord thy God*' by interpreting it to mean, Heaven forbid, '*thou shalt hate the Lord*'? The text bears no other interpretation but that Moses took a Cushite or Ethiopian woman ... After Moses married Zipporah he took another wife, an Ethiopian woman ... It is not our business to pry into his motives! He knew what he was about ... Had Moses separated himself completely from woman, adopting a life of celibacy as the ancients averred, Moses would not have been the most perfect man that had ever walked the world. Our Sages have stated that "whoever is greater than his fellows, his impulses are greater than his." His

natural vitality and activities had not become weakened at eighty and even at a
hundred. How can you argue that Moses
became a celibate! He was no Franciscan,
Augustine or Carmelite monk.

The Talmud points out, King Saul was called
"a Cushite" and so was Zedekiah, as a term of
endearment. (Moed Katan 16b). "Black" in Hebrew is a synonym for lovely.

After the death of Sarah, Abraham, our Father, took another woman to his tent. Genesis
25:1: "*Then again Abraham took a wife, and
her name was Keturah.*" In his notes to Targum
Sheyni, the scholar Paullus Cassel points out
that the hoopoo bird or cock of the woods, who
comes to inform King Solomon of the realm of
the Queen of Sheba, has flown from its capital
city, Kitor. The name is related to the Hebrew
word for incense, the smoke of incense, keto-
rot. It refers to the frankincense for which Saba
or Sheba, was famous. Keturah too, is from the
land of Sheba, the kingdom in the south of Ara-
bia and Ethiopia across the waterway. The next
lines of Genesis 25, confirm it, for her children
populate that area: "*Then again Abraham took a
wife, and her name was Keturah. And she bore
him Zimran, and Jokashn, and Medan, and Midian, and Ishbak, and Shuah. And Jokshan begat
Sheba and Dedan.*"

Was not only Moses, our Teacher, but Abraham, our Father, blessed with a black wife? If

Keturah was not black, certainly some of her children were the black children not of Ham but Abraham. This is Scripture, Torah!

But what does Torah mean by the following? *"And Abraham gave all that he had unto Isaac. But to the sons of the Abraham's concubines, Abraham gave gifts and sent them away from Isaac his son, while he yet lived, eastward, into the east country."*

Rabbi Samuel, the son of Nachmani, in Midrash Ha-Godol quotes Abraham as follows: "'My son Isaac is young and every nation and tongue that will subjugate him and his sons will be driven to Hell. Therefore, go and stand in the East. So long as Isaac's sons are subjugated to the nations, remain in your place.

"'But when you hear that they are dwelling securely and tranquilly, come and serve them so that you merit the table of Messiah.' And it is concerning them, that he [Job] says, *"Look at the roads of Tamar, the pathways of Sheba, wait for them."* (Job 6:19.) Sheba is none other than the sons of Keturah. As it is written, *"And Jokshan gave birth to Sheba."* (Genesis 25:3) And they dwelt in their place until King Solomon arose. And Israel was living securely. As it is written, *"And Judah and Israel dwelt safely, every man under his vine and his fig tree, from Dan even to Beersheba, all the days of Solomon."* (I Kings 5:5). They thought that he was King Messiah and of them came to serve him.

For it is written, "*The Queen of Sheba heard of Solomon's fame.*" Rabbi Yochanan says, "He who says that [the expression] *Queen of Sheba* is a woman is only mistaken. You should not read *Queen of Sheba* but the *Kingdom of Sheba.*" For the difference between Queen, *malchat*, in Hebrew, and Kingdom, *malchoot*, is purely a matter of vowels and so the letters (without vowels) can be read either way. That is the whole kingdom of Sheba came in the days of Solomon to serve the Israelites, for it says, '*for the sake of the Lord.*' What does it refer to, '*for the sake of the Lord.*' The Hebrew of I Kings 10:1, which is usually read, '*When the Queen of Sheba heard the fame of Solomon concerning the Lord, she came to prove him,*' can be read, '*When the Kingdom of Sheba heard the fame of Solomon, for the sake of the Lord, it came to prove him.*'"

Why did the lords of Sheba come? Rabbi Samuel says, "For the sake of that thing which Abraham transmitted to them—that the Holy One, blessed be He, was destined to reveal His Kingdom to Israel and to settle them securely. When they saw that he [Solomon] was not the King Messiah, immediately, '*She turned around to her land*' (II Chronicles 9:12). That means they (and their queen) returned to their place. And they are destined to come in the days of King Messiah when he will be revealed, soon, in our days. As it says, '*Dust, clouds of camels shall cover you. Dromedaries of Median and Ephah. They all shall come from Sheba'* (Isaiah 60:6).

Does the world wait for the children of Sheba, the golden clouds of their camels, to signal Messiah?

Notions of a fixed world are nonsense. The continents shift like stories, bump, nuzzle one another, break off, fuse. Place is relative and why not time too? The nose leads on.

"A melody of sweetness ran through the luminous air …ineffable delights …while I went on among so many first fruits of eternal pleasure, in suspense, and desiring still more happiness, before us, like an ascending flame, the air under those green boughs." Dante sings of his steps through paradise.

The shining flanks of a woman disappear in the foliage of scripture, one thread joins another, singing, burbling, until you stroke in the broad waters of four primitive rivers flowing into one.

The guide, great Cassuto, in his commentary on Genesis maps a world without rain. "A river flowed out of Eden to water the garden, that is, the garden was watered by a river emanating from a spring, and not by rain … Alas, when Man sinned, we lost the blessing of these springs. The Lord punished us and decreed that from now on moisture would descend from above. When we behaved, obeyed, the clouds would open, and rain would fall in season. When we broke the laws, His heavens would shut tight. O the dry, dead dust.

"And the Lord God planted a garden in Eden, in the east:

"And there He put the man ... A river flowed out of Eden to water the garden, and from there it divided." Everywhere through shining vegetation, the sound of water, rushing, eddying, gushing up from the earth. According to the guide, "The etymological meaning of the name, Eden," is "a place that is well watered throughout."

Others have known this place, its portages, "The ancient people of the East, and not of the East alone, used to tell many stories about the primeval rivers ..." Is the source of the rivers, which flow through Babylon, Assyria, surge through Egypt, bubble from Jerusalem, the same? The guide refers to the chart of cosmogony, the birth of worlds. Geography but the handmaiden of its cataclysms, here the cataclysmic event is sin, a single bite in an apple.

In the midst of the rivers of the world flows the memory of the Mother Brook, "the Divine River" destined to become a source of blessing in the Messianic era, which, as the guide says, "May refer to the renewal of the bliss of the garden of Eden by means of the stream that will flow from the site of the Temple."

The river of Messiah flowed, will flow, from the Temple walls—little gasping Gihon, under the iron grates, between the chisel marks of

Hezekiah's men, pumping, gasping, roaring to the end of the earth. Stones of gold buckle from the earth, rubies, diamonds, sapphires, trinkets in the pavement as hosts march to a throne. Say not the *Queen of Sheba* but the *Kingdom of Sheba*, ah rainbow!

Not in this century. No, Israel has a running nose, fever, *kadoches*. The whole world *kadoches, kadoches, kadoches*. Standing at the street corners, crossroads, abusing each other. "Still let me sleep, embracing dreams—" but not "in vain." The watcher does not fear "the day's disdain."

Slowly, the boat glides to the gate. Laughter, the golden happy laughter of the Holy One peels across the waters. The bells tinkle on the ankles of the princess and I draw from the honeyed stream, my shawl.

Where's Maishe?

What was Maishe doing in the park?

A truant, a missing space in Hebrew School. Up and down the aisles a lady rages with silver hair, a wiry bundle of crackling sterling threads, shooting sparks of fury, smacking her splintered pointer on the coffin of a vacant desk. "I'll kill him," she screamed. "When I get my hands on him, I'll tear his arms off."

The assembly of boys and girls rocks back and forth, humming fearfully their "*Aleph Bays*," reciting by rote and with only fitful gleams of understanding from the purple *siddurs* spread open under their noses. They hop from consonant to consonant, squinting at the jiggling balls of the vowels in little heaps of one, two, three and the tiny T crosses and slashes. Here are the pious exclamations of forefathers, limbs severed, lying in baskets, through the synagogues of Germany. These pages are the arrangements of petitions by sages of Palestine who coughed and sang as the Roman centurions scraped the flesh off their backs with fiery rakes, heated pokers. The sticky eyes of the children avoid the empty seat in their midst, its black, gleaming board of scratched and lacquered oak, syrupy as a honey pot. The comfort of the pages moving dizzily under their fingers to the chant rising in succession, desk by desk, is in their drone, which laps at the sharp edge of the teacher's scream and seeks to blunt it.

Maishe Ostropol is missing.

Under the thick glasses of the old woman teaching them, one optical glass glued to the next, a convex sandwich of transparent plates bulging from the silver wire hooked over her nose and to the back of her pink, now gleaming, ears, the absence is not apparent at first. As the children have discovered, she flails helplessly many feet off her target when she must locate a malefactor by sight alone. It is those rose-tipped, burning ears which are infallible. The slightest peep and whirring from the blackboard, she has noted the source, sent her ragged chalk flying—a torpedo to the offending cheek, a red mark of scorn burned under the gun powder of white dust.

The hour creeps toward its close on the Arabic face of the clock at the back of the classroom before the Hebrew recitation has reached even the first seat in the row of seven chairs, the sixth and last row across from the door over by the window where the missing child is assigned to sit.

What they are reading between the stiff purple boards of the *siddurs* handed out in the balmy days of September in the middle of holidays, sweetmeats, and heavy meals fizzing with orange seltzer, ginger ale, vanilla soda, has never been explained. A year or two ago they mastered the consonants and vowels of Hebrew in the Ashkenazi lip, vocalization of Roman Palestine, and now they skip from one incomprehensible paragraph of Hebrew print to the other in a hopscotch dictated by the whim of the old lady nodding in the maple office chair behind the teacher's desk.

One by one the children's attention slips away. Their thoughts wander over the maps of the Holy Land pulled down by the right-hand blackboard of the classroom or the great poster of tree stamps which marks the progress of thirty boys and girls in planting the desolation of an ancient land but an infant state—the greenery of a dark and endless forest.

It is through the stamps of trees stuck to the poster, the rows of trees budding, pushing root through the slate of the blackboard, the boys and girls slip into enchanted arbors, join the bands of Joshua, the Maccabees, the ring of dancing girls under Mount Zion. Only yesterday, Maishe Ostropol was foremost among them, taking the ass of Balaam by the bit as it crouched before the wall and angel of the Lord, saddling the beast under the eyes of an astonished wizard and galloping for freedom. Racing down the hills of Moab, Maishe spurred the talking animal over stone fence, boulders, falling timbers, to the Jordan's ford.

Such are the byways of children in *cheder*. The trick is to crane your eyes with a soundless shift of shoulders over the back of the boy or girl just in front when the recitation comes to him, her, note the page and follow the child in front's finger to the line incanted.

The talking ass is a dangerous paramour. He carries you off all the while, telling tales.

How Moses has an Ethiopian girlfriend. How Aaron … How Miriam … How they … How … How … They are splashing in the stream about Maishe's ankles, kneecaps, as the chalk explodes against his forehead. "Idiot!" Leaving a red welt, "Idiot!" that marks him in the night, under the street lamps, like Cain.

Reviews of previous fiction by Mark Jay Mirsky

About Thou Worm Jacob

One of the old rude joyous story-teller come newly to life. In *Thou Worm Jacob*, his Jews—the ten saddest Jews in the environs of Boston—are created with humor, pride, despair, and a kind of ancient love. To me the book is amazing.

John Hawkes

Your strange eloquence is beautifully sustained through one weird history after another, your humor seems to me uniquely right, you never make a false move as far as I can see; and the greatest impression the whole thing makes on my mind is of piety—piety about the past, and about the passing of things, that is unsentimental and poetically just.

Howard Nemerov

Mark Mirsky is a miracle worker. He has the tears of comedy, the laughter of tragedy, and the speaking voice of life—all in a stylization that lets us know instantly we are in the presence of a great teller of tales. I hope never to miss a word he writes.

John Ciardi

Here is a book above the ephemera of best sellers. I say, long may it be read!

Francis Russell, *The Christian Science Monitor*

Thou Worm Jacob is a pure comic novel with a serious communiqué from the author, in which he laments the passing of the old-world, and other-worldly Jew. Not other-worldly in the sense of despising money and what it can buy and do for you, but in the sense of a timeless and space less cultural inheritance whose last shards huddle together …

Anne Bernays, *Boston Sunday Globe*,

This first novel is an exploding star of talent, nostalgia and comedy.

Los Angeles Times

Proceedings of the Rabble

Mirsky piles public outrage on private injustice; satirizes America as a gathering of vermin and takes his title from the Olympian rat, Jonathan Swift, the man who was "so enormously satisfied with the procedure of human things," that he thought of preparing "A Modest Defense of the Proceedings of the Rabble in All Ages." Mirsky's defense is a cheer for politics, our national psychodrama where everyone has fun being the rat he is. And for every ton of spleen in this novel, there's an ounce of truth that makes it grimly, stinkingly good.

What breaks through Mirsky's satire is a terrible sense of people as grotesque, doomed to weakness or rage and fighting to get away from themselves, from that awful truth so gently put by Pogo: "We have met the enemy and they are us."

Josephine Hendin: *New York Times*: June 20, 1971

America in ruins. Minds shattered. Pigs, rats and vultures picking over the mountains of garbage in the streets of New York. A powerful political movement, dressed in black shirts controls limp minds without ever defining its stands, left or right. Madness in subways and television … And through it all, unlikely and hazardous, as it sounds, Mark Mirsky shines through his wicked laughter, blazes in his jagged, sensuous nightmare prose …

Mirsky's writing is some dream process for both writer and reader. It is also extremely well-made, reading often like a prose poem. His flashing montages fit with one another if you take your time in the labyrinth …

Mirsky has seized upon repressed sexual desire, violence, media madness and a vision of the Big Lie, and made it not only frightening and hysterical but also funny. His is an apocalyptic landscape shoddy perhaps only for its comic-strip extremism, and his characters are the crazy extensions of George Wallace, Walter

Cronkite, William Westmoreland, Richard Nixon and the editor of the National Enquirer.

His tale grows to fable, where human beings turn into animals ... drawn into the final doomsday convention of the Continentals. Religion and politics' dance inseparable from each other as the vision of ultimate power simmers and sours in the eyes of Middle America.

Mark Mirsky is a scary new writer, capable of jolts and flights to turn both the head and the stomach. He is Swiftian in his twisted prophecy.

William Gallo, *The Rocky Mountain News*

This compelling novel about private and public madness pulls the reader into a whirlpool of insanity and bestial vision of horror and doom ... It reads like a nightmare delivered intact.

Publisher's Weekly

Blue Hill Avenue

New and Recommended in *The New York Sunday Times,* November 19, 1972

Mark Mirsky's new book is many things but it is primarily literature. To me the Jewish experience is, when it is not in a book, a closed book. Mr. Mirsky makes it universal, but first one is aware of the medium, the rich graceful strong language, the awareness of the need to make reality real through coaxing a pattern out of it. This is words magnificently employed. This is literature.

Anthony Burgess

Citied in *The Boston Globe*, July 21, 2009 as among the *100 Essential Books about New England*.

The Red Adam

A densely plotted, magically written novel that reminds one of how inextricably tied love, sex and mortality in fact are. Few contemporary Jewish American fictions are so thoroughly haunted by the divine, so energized by the juxtaposition of the evil and the divine, and so utterly committed to the creative act in both its reverence and its comedy.

Sanford Pinsker: *The Jewish Post and Opinion*:

In a section of Mark Mirsky's *The Red Adam*, we read of a Golem—Jewish mystical tradition's artificial man—created when a violent storm, blowing through the broken window of a New England study, blows hundreds of documents together in the from the Talmud and the Kabbalah along with a powerful dose of Jonathan Edwards, the great Puritan divine. This paper golem its function more metaphorical than actual, is not, as it happens the clay monster that spells havoc for a small New England town: that we read of a little later. Nevertheless, the range of quotations with which its genesis is interleaved takes the measure of Mr. Mirsky's creation ... Mr. Mirsky, transplanting Jewish legend to the New World, has indeed been mindful of the medieval formulae: he has made his golem from virgin soil, creating with *The Red Adam* a new genre— Jewish American gothic.

Saul Rosenberg: *The Jewish Forward*: July 13, 1990

About the Author

Mark Jay Mirsky was born in Boston and grew up in the Dorchester, Mattapan, Roxbury districts, which border Franklin Park to the east, north and south. Attending Boston Public Latin, Harvard College and Stanford University, Mr. Mirsky has previously published four novels, *Thou Worm Jacob*, *Proceedings of the Rabble*, *Blue Hill Avenue*, *The Red Adam*, a collection of short stories called *The Secret Table*, and several books of criticism: *My Search for the Messiah*; *Dante, Eros, and Kabbalah*; *The Absent Shakespeare*; and his latest, *The Drama in Shakespeare's Sonnets: A Satire to Decay*. He is the coeditor of *Rabbinic Fantasies* (Yale University Press) *The Jews of Pinsk Volumes 1 & 2* (Stanford University Press), and the editor of Robert Musil's *Diaries* in English (Basic Books). He founded the journal *FICTION* in 1972 with Donald Barthelme, Jane DeLynn, and Max and Marianne Frisch and has been its editor-in-chief up to the present. A Professor of English at The City College of New York, he has served as its chairperson and director of Jewish Studies. His reviews and articles on architecture and literature have appeared in *The New York Sunday Times*, *The Washington*

Post, The International Herald Tribune, The Massachusetts Review, Partisan Review, The Progressive, Haaretz, and numerous other publications. His play *Mother Hubbard's Cupboard* was performed at the Fringe Festival in 2007 and is posted on www.indietheaternow.com

An autobiographical essay published in 1999 on Mark Jay Mirsky can be found in Volume 30 of Gale's *Contemporary Authors,* and a chapter is dedicated to him in Jules Chametzky's collection *Out of Brownsville.* His latest novel about Boston lost in the 1960s is called *Franklin Park Puddingstone,* and is available in print as well as e-book form.

His articles appear on the FICTION website, www.fictioninc.com and his blog www.markmirsky.com

24949596R00161

Made in the USA
Middletown, DE
11 October 2015